A Present for Yanya

A Present for Yanya

by **PEGGY MANN** and **KATICA PRUSINA**

Illustrated by Douglas Gorsline

Random House New York

Copyright © 1975 by Peggy Mann and Katica Prusina. Illustrations Copyright © 1975 by Random House, Inc. All rights reserved under International and Pan-American Copyright Conventions. Published in the United States by Random House, Inc., New York, and simultaneously in Canada by Random House of Canada Limited, Toronto.

Library of Congress Cataloging in Publication Data

Mann, Peggy. A present for Yanya. SUMMARY: In Yugoslavia not long after World War II, a young girl dreams of owning the doll she sees in a market window, knowing her family can never afford to buy it. [1. Dolls — Fiction. 2. Yugoslavia — Fiction.] I. Prusina, Katica, joint author. II. Gorsline, Douglas W., 1913- illus. III. Title. PZ7.M31513Pr [Fic] 75-8074. ISBN 0-394-82425-3. ISBN 0-394-92425-8 (lib. bdg.)

Manufactured in the United States of America   1 2 3 4 5 6 7 8 9 0

To
Ivka Herceg Prusina
and to
Edna Brand Mann

A Present for Yanya

This is a true story.
It is set in Yugoslavia
in the years following
World War II.

1

Yanya woke up early, even before the crowing of the cocks.

She lay looking out the wide-open window at the fading stars and wriggled her toes with impatience. If only it were time to get up.

Today she was going to the market town of Orasja where she would see the strange and beautiful Moslem women who wore veils across their faces so that only their eyes showed. She had never been to the market town before.

The moon moved from behind clouds and its brightness fell through the window. She could tell time by the stretch of moonlight across the floor. It was nearly three in the morning.

Suddenly Yanya kicked back the blanket. She would get ready and be waiting by the time Mama opened her eyes.

Quietly, she started to dress. She had only one skirt, one blouse, one set of underwear. But her mother had washed and ironed them all yesterday, so it was like putting on a special set of clothes. Carefully, she combed and braided her hair, tying each brown braid at the end with a string.

She wished that her hair were beautiful and shining blond. Or, at the very least, black like Mama's. (Sometimes, when Mama braided Yanya's hair, she complained about its mousy-brown color. Yanya would always reply indignantly, "Well, I like it the way it is!" But actually she did not like it at all.)

Today, however, she had something that would make her beautiful.

One evening she had watched Lisa, a neighbor's daughter, getting ready to go out with her young man. Lisa took a scrap of red crepe paper, spit on it, and rubbed it over her cheeks and lips to give them more color. All the big girls did this, Lisa said. Shyly, Yanya had asked whether she might have a small piece.

She had hidden the precious red crepe paper between the wooden bedboard and the straw on which she slept. She knelt now, took out the folded square of paper, and wet a corner with spit. Lisa had looked into a mirror when putting on the color. But Yanya had no mirror. At least, none that she was permitted to use. The only mirror in the house was a small cracked one which belonged to Papa. It was left from the days before the war. When Papa was not using the mirror for his morning shave, he kept it hidden in a box underneath his bed. There was a strict rule in the house. No one was to use Papa's mirror. The reason was clear. If his mirror were accidentally broken, Papa might cut his handsome face when shaving.

Sometimes, in the daylight, if she wanted to see her face, Yanya tacked some newspaper over the bedroom window. Then she would go out in the backyard to look at her reflection in the sunlit window glass.

However, since the sun would not be up before they started off to market, Yanya rubbed on the crepe-paper red by feeling the shape of her cheeks and lips. Then she realized that in her excitement she had forgotten to wash her face. If she washed it now the red might smear all over. But she did tiptoe into the kitchen to rinse her mouth.

Suddenly, the faint crowing of a rooster sounded from the distance. It was promptly picked up by other roosters in other backyards throughout the town, and the darkness soon echoed with their cries.

Mama would be getting up.

Yanya remained in the kitchen—for Mama did not allow anyone to watch her while she dressed. Except, of course, for the baby, Pero, who slept in a cradle next to her bed. But Pero was only nine months old.

While she waited Yanya took from the shelf the bowl of goat cheese and the round loaf of black bread which Mama had baked last week. It was wrapped in a linen cloth to keep it fresh. She set the bread and cheese on the table and looked at them. But she could not eat. She was too excited.

Then Mama walked into the kitchen. "So," she said. "Up already."

Yanya nodded, smiling, waiting for Mama to say something about her beautiful red cheeks and lips. Then she realized that in the moonlight the red would not show.

Mama shoved wood and kindling into the stove, lit it, put some milk and two pots of water on to boil. "Get breakfast for your papa and me," she said. "And change the baby." Then she went out into the backyard to feed the rabbits and chickens and to pick the vegetables they would sell to the Moslem women.

Yanya knew very well why Mama had agreed to bring her along this morning. It was Registration Day and she should, by rights, be taking Yanya to register for school, which opened in two weeks. But Mama had told her that she could not go to school. Not yet. And Yanya understood the reason.

Her two older brothers, Marko and Ivo, would soon be coming home in order to go to school. They could no longer hire themselves out to farmers as they did during the summertime. And Papa was still unable to get out of bed and go to work. So it was up to Mama to earn the money and grow the food that they lived on. And it was up to Yanya to do all the work that Mama did not have time to do.

But understanding the reason she could not go to school did not help too much. She still felt an angry bitterness swell inside her every time she thought about all the other children her age going off to register for school.

"You'll have fun at home," Mama had said. "A lot of children *wish* they could stay home from school."

Yanya had not answered.

After a moment her mother had said, "Well, to show you how much I need you—I'll even take you with me on market day."

And Yanya had let out a yelp of joy.

During the two years they'd lived here in Bosnjaci, she had never once been outside the town. Now she would not only be going to another town eight kilometers away, she would be traveling back to Bosnia. Bosnia, the province in which she'd been born. Bosnia, the only place she felt she would ever belong.

When the milk simmered, Yanya took it off the stove. When the water in the two pots boiled, she spooned ground coffee into one, put three eggs in the other. And, when breakfast was ready, she carried

---

it in and set it carefully on the chair by Papa's side of the bed.

Then she shook her father gently by the shoulder. He grunted.

"Breakfast, Papa," Yanya said. "It's early this morning because Mama and I are going to the market." She felt very proud saying this sentence. "Mama and I have to leave very soon. So wake up and eat before your breakfast gets cold."

Groaning and grumbling, Papa sat up and Yanya placed the pillows behind his back. The Germans had beaten and tortured Papa in the prison camp. Although he had come home some months ago, the pains and aches were still with him.

"So today's the big day," Papa said. She could see him smile in the moon-softened darkness.

"Yes, Papa." Suddenly, for some reason, she kissed him on the forehead. Then she felt embarrassed. She had hardly ever kissed her father before. She hurried over to the cradle, picked up the sleeping Pero, and carried him to her bed. The baby began to cry as she unwound his long, wet diaper.

"You stay there, Pero," she told him severely. "Don't roll off the bed!" She ran into the kitchen, wet a piece of cloth, and returned to wipe the baby clean and pat him dry.

His cries had turned now to chortles of delight as he kicked and punched at the air. He enjoyed his freedom. It seemed a shame to have to swaddle him up again. But she and Mama would be away all morning. And since Papa could not look after the baby, the only thing to do was to bind him tightly so he could not scratch his face, or pull the blanket over his head.

She put a soft diaper between his legs, then took the long narrow linen cloth, wound it round the baby's waist, around and down till it reached his ankles, and around and up to encase his arms and

chest. Then she tied the ends securely. She lifted the now screaming Pero and laid him back in his cradle. Then she picked up his night-wet diapers, ran out to the backyard, and washed them clean in the wooden pail beside the well.

When she returned to the kitchen Mama was finishing breakfast. "The sun will be up soon," Mama said. "We must hurry. Collect the eggs, Yanya. I'll nurse the baby. Then we'll be off."

Yanya ran through the backyard to the chicken coop. She liked the feel of the dew-wet grass against her bare feet. But she hesitated before entering the chicken coop. The moon had gone again behind clouds. She knew the coop would be very black inside. It frightened her—the dank smell, the squawking chickens flapping against her legs in the darkness. She was always certain an angry hen would nip her as she felt underneath the warm body for an egg.

But each separate egg might be worth as much as two *dinars*. And the family's only source of income was the money made each market day from the sale of the vegetables and eggs. She took a deep breath, opened the door, and entered the chicken coop.

Like a blind girl she groped about in the darkness. A hen flapped down from its roost, straight into her face. She screamed. But she kept on feeling through the straw, trying to murmur in a friendly way to the fat hens to show that she was not afraid.

When she emerged she had seventeen fresh-laid eggs in her wicker basket. One hundred eighty-nine more were in the storehouse—eggs that had been collected during the week. How many eggs did they have altogether? She started counting on her fingers, but she got confused. Perhaps when she finally went to school she would learn some magic way of quickly adding up the eggs.

As she hurried across to the storage shed, the first streaks of daylight were seeping through the sky. She stopped by the herb garden, picked some basil, and rubbed it between her hands as she had seen the older girls do. It smelled like sweet perfume. Then she plucked one of the roses by the door of the toolshed and stuck it in her hair.

When she entered the kitchen, carrying a basket which held over two hundred eggs, she felt almost as old as Lisa. And almost as beautiful.

She heard Papa calling out in the bedroom, "Hurry up, woman! It's almost four o'clock. You'll be late to the market."

Papa, Yanya reflected, was very fond of giving out orders like a general from his bed. Mama never answered back. But she generally gave him a hard look which said more than many words. Yanya, however, always replied politely, "Yes, Papa." But in her mind she muttered many bad words. She wondered what Papa had been like before the Germans took him away to the prison camp. Had he worked hard then, like other men in the village? She could not remember, and she did not dare to ask.

Mama now hurried into the kitchen dressed in the black wool skirt and long-sleeved black blouse that had been worn by *her* mother before the old lady died. Since it was market day, Mama also wore a flowered apron and a bright scarf on her head.

"Are you ready?" Mama said. "Good. You carry the cabbages."

Mama herself took two baskets, one filled with eggs, the other with vegetables, and went outside.

Yanya, proud at being able to carry her own basket to market, took the cabbages and went to the door.

"Good-by, Papa," she called.

"Good-by, girl," he shouted from the bedroom. "Bring back lots of money." Then he added, "And have a good time."

"I will, Papa."

Dawn had now paled the sky. She could see quite clearly.

Mama was waiting by the roadway. Yanya hurried to her.

Suddenly Mama screamed.

Yanya dropped her basket in terror.

Mama pointed. "Your face! What happened?"

"Why, Mama? What's wrong?"

"You're flaming red. You have the fever! Go right back and get to bed!"

"No, Mama," said Yanya, highly insulted. "It's . . . I . . . It was just to be pretty." And, haltingly, she told her mother about the red crepe paper.

Mama added to the redness with a hard slap across Yanya's cheek. "You'll go about the way God made you! Now march straight back to the house and wash off that color at once!"

So Yanya, with tears streaking her red cheeks, returned to the kitchen.

"Who's there?" Papa called out sharply from his bed.

"It's just me, Papa," Yanya said in a very small voice. "I . . . forgot to wash my face."

2

At first it was fine—trudging along the dirt road past fields of wheat which stretched back golden to the far horizon . . . past shepherds who had brought their fat, baaing sheep to drink at a roadside stream . . . past green fields speckled with bright sunflowers . . . past vineyards climbing up the hillsides.

At first it was exciting.

But after two hours the sun had become very hot. The basket had become very heavy. And Yanya had asked at least five times, "Mama, when will we get there?"

If Mama answered her at all, it was only to reply tartly, "We'll get there when we get there!" But most of the time she was too busy to pay any attention to Yanya. She was busy talking to Manda the Widow, who was walking with them.

Yanya reflected bitterly that Manda certainly did not go about with the face God had given her. Indeed, she had already stopped four times to take her compact from her apron pocket. She would snap it open, look at herself in the small mirror, and wipe the sweat from her face. Then she patted on powder, and applied red color to her lips from a tiny tube. Once she stopped, lit a match, blew it out, and rubbed the charcoal matchstick over her light eyebrows.

And each time that Manda stopped for such repairs, Mama would watch and laugh a little and joke about Manda's beauty.

Yanya herself did not think the widow very beautiful. But evidently the men who passed by on the road or in carts found Manda highly attractive. They laughed with her and teased her and threw insults that were really compliments.

When the men came, Mama was quiet. But she seemed to enjoy Manda's popularity. Yanya, on the other hand, felt embarrassed to be walking with the widow who, she felt, laughed too loudly and talked too much.

Presently, they reached the crest of a hill. And there beyond the Sava River lay Orasja, the market town.

Yanya gasped. It looked like a picture in a story-book Lisa had once lent her.

The river was wide and green, flecked with sun-light. Coming across it, made small by distance, was a long, flat barge. And downstream there was the wooden wheel of a water mill.

Across the river rose the town. The houses looked, from where she stood, like toys set out along crooked streets. And in the center of town, a slender tower rose against the sky.

Yanya tugged at her mother's apron, wanting to ask about the tower. But Mama was still chattering with Manda and paid no attention.

They went down the hill toward the boat, walking slowly now for the road was steep, lined with ruts from the wheels of many wagons, and slippery with mud.

Then they climbed the grassy dike. Beyond, close to the small stone pier, was a café. Men were sitting at wooden tables beneath the willow trees.

Suddenly Yanya discovered that she was very thirsty.

"Mama!" She pulled again at the flowered apron, this time so hard that her mother looked down, surprised.

"I'm thirsty, Mama! My throat feels covered with dust inside. Could we have a lemonade at the café?"

"That place is only for men," her mother said sharply. "What do you think!" Then she added, her voice softer now, "When we get to the market you can have a drink. There's water in the park."

Yanya nodded. But she trudged on across the field feeling defiant now. Why must women go thirsty while the men relaxed in comfort, drinking beneath the willow trees? Women walked just as far, grew just as hot, longed just as much for a cooling lemonade. Why did her mother accept such unfairness as though it were a rule laid down by God?

They crowded onto the small pier, and Yanya soon forgot her indignation as she watched the melee of men, women, carts, cows, sheep, pigs, and goats waiting to board the riverboat. Several women held small babies, but Yanya noted with pride that she was the only child.

First the horse-drawn carts creaked along the gangplank and lined up in the center of the wide barge. Then all the people with animals paraded up the plank. They tied their cows, goats, and pigs to the carts or the boat railing. Finally the boatman signaled all others who waited, and they crowded aboard. Yanya clung hard to her mother's arm so she would not be pushed into the water.

They found a place near the railing where she watched wide-eyed as the two boatmen drew in the gangplank and shoved off. By pulling hand-over-hand on a heavy rope stretched across the river, they managed somehow to move the heavy barge.

She wanted to ask her mother how this was possible. But Mama was never good at answering questions. Indeed, Mama felt that questions should not be asked. Perhaps Papa would explain to her when she got home how two men could move a boat which held over two hundred people, plus cows and horses and heavy carts.

As the barge slid out into the river the cows on board started mooing . . . the sheep and goats baaing and bleating . . . the pigs squealing . . . the chickens screeching and squawking as they flapped about in market baskets and slatted boxes. Did they sense, Yanya wondered, that they were all on their way to being sold for food?

Suddenly, as she stared down into the river waters, her mind was filled with a terrible memory, long-forgotten.

She *had* been to this river before. Once on an autumn afternoon her oldest brother, Marko, had taken her with him when he was a cowherd. They had just moved to the province of Slavonia, and Marko had found a job for the summer tending the neighbors' cows.

She remembered squatting by the banks of the slow-moving Sava as the cows munched grass at the river's edge. She was building a castle of mud, sticks, and small stones.

Upstream she spied a fallen tree, its branches dragging in the water. She ran to the tree to gather more sticks and twigs for her castle. Suddenly she saw, caught in the branches, a body floating face down. A soldier. The sleeve of his uniform had been ripped away. She screamed.

Yanya never went again to play by the river, for her brother had told her later that it was not uncommon to see the body of a dead soldier floating in the Sava.

She felt chilled now as she stared down into the shadowy depths of the river. The war had been over for many months. Still, an undiscovered body might come drifting downstream. Were those weeds moving slowly far below? Or shadows? Or what? She shivered and turned away to stare at the opposite shore.

As they got off the boat an old man was standing by the gangplank to collect the passage money—five dinars per person. He smiled at Yanya. "I haven't seen *you* before," he said.

She smiled back. She could think of nothing to say to this kind old man, so she told him, "My name is Yanya." Then she hurried after her mother.

"Have a good day, little Yanya," he called.

She turned and waved to him. And somehow she felt much better.

Excitement mounted within her as they climbed up the muddy road. The houses in Orasja were tall, some two or even three stories high. They were made of stone or gray brick. None was painted. And each was hidden from the street by high iron or wooden fences. The long wooden shutters on the windows were closed. The long wooden front doors were also closed. The perfect setting, Yanya reflected, for the mysterious Moslem women who lived there. Like the women, the houses too were veiled.

It was hard to believe that this market town lay only eight kilometers from her own town of Bosnjaci. It seemed to be in another world. In her town each house was fresh-painted every spring—yellow, pink, pale green, or deep blue. The shutters were painted in contrasting shades. And bright flower pots lined the window sills. In the warm weather, shutters and doors always stood open. Women sat out on wooden benches by the roadside under the walnut trees, chatting, gossiping, doing their embroidery. The dirt roads and the grassy sidewalks overflowed with children playing and geese, chickens, and ducks parading.

It was, she knew, a friendly-looking town, even though she had as yet found no friends.

"Hurry, Yanya!" her mother scolded. "You'll get lost."

They turned the corner and came upon a brick-paved street lined with shops. At the very first shop window Yanya stopped and stared.

A doll was there, staring back at her—a doll more beautiful than anything she had ever imagined. It was tall, half the size of Yanya herself, with large blue eyes edged by long lashes. Black curly hair hung down to her shoulders. She had red cheeks and a

small red mouth, faintly smiling.

And her dress! It was made of soft red silk with a fringe of lace at the cuffs. She had small white socks, shiny black shoes. And her arms were stretched out— toward Yanya.

Somehow Yanya did not feel surprised to see such a doll. She had expected to find something magical in this market town of the Moslem women. She was not even surprised that the doll should be in a shop window surrounded by iron hoes, wooden troughs, pails and pots, dustpans and brooms. Everything was lightly powdered with dust, even the doll.

"Do you want me to buy you?" Yanya whispered. She and the doll smiled at each other—the same very small smile, as though both knew how impossible this was. Yanya had never in her life owned even a pair of shoes. How then could there ever be money enough to buy such a splendid doll?

"Bad girl!" Her mother grabbed her arm, jerked her around. "Didn't I tell you to stay with me? I was halfway to the marketplace before I missed you. This is a crowded place. You can get lost here."

Yanya trotted along after her mother, who was holding hard to her arm.

But in her mind she whispered, "Good-by, beautiful doll. Don't be lonesome. I'll come to visit you later—on my way home."

3

For a long while—several hours perhaps—Yanya
did not think a single thought about the doll. There
were too many other exciting things to look at, to
listen to.

When they arrived at the market square she understood at once why her mother always liked to be
there early. Those who came first could settle in the
center of the square. The late arrivals had to display
their wares in the side streets leading off the square.
But few people went to the side streets to shop, for all
the color and life and laughter flowed and jumbled
in the square itself.

Yanya and her mother found a place on the curb
in the center of the busiest section of all. Some of the
peasants rented low wooden tables on which they

spread out their tomatoes, potatoes, cabbages, cheeses, and such. Some, like Manda and Mama, kept their vegetables and eggs in market baskets. But many others arranged their produce in piles on the dusty brick roadway.

Yanya longed to go off exploring, to stop at each shop window. But before she had even asked for permission Mama said to her firmly, "Now you stay right here, girl! The crowds will be coming soon and I don't want to lose you again."

There was a small park in the center of the square, and far to the left stood the strange, tall tower she had seen from the other side of the river. Its silver dome glinted in the sunlight. Perhaps it was the castle of a Moslem princess.

Then she turned and saw the princess—walking straight toward her. A slender figure wearing flowing silken robes and high-heeled blue shoes. Her hair was covered by a shiny blue shawl, her face by a lacy veil.

She stopped directly in front of Yanya. Her voice was soft and strangely accented. "*Mala* [little girl], will you sell me some eggs?"

Yanya could only nod.

Her mother cut in quickly. "How many, pretty madame?"

But the Turkish princess continued to address Yanya. "Twenty, please, mala," she said. "Are they fresh?"

"Oh, y–yes, madame," Yanya stammered. "I gathered them myself this morning."

Then the princess lifted her veil, drew it back over her scarf. Her eyes were large, black, and lustrous. Her skin was pale, the true sign of royalty, for such a woman had obviously never worked in the fields under the burning sun. Her lips were scarlet red. She wore golden loop earrings, and a necklace of jewels.

"Would you pick them out for me?" the princess said to Yanya.

Again her mother cut in. "Twenty eggs will be sixty dinars, madame."

Yanya had heard her mother report many times on the bargaining and haggling that went on at the market. It was therefore expected by buyer and seller that the first price mentioned would be far too high. But the princess merely nodded and held out a cardboard box toward Yanya. "I like large, pale eggs, mala. Will you put them in here?"

Carefully Yanya counted out the eggs, avoiding those which still had the fuzz of chicken feathers stuck to them.

"Please hold them for me," the princess said, handing Yanya the box of eggs. She took a lace handkerchief from her pocket, untied it, and counted sixty dinars. She held out the money to Yanya, who reached so eagerly for the coins that she dropped the box of eggs.

"Fool!" her mother screamed out.

Yanya stared down, appalled, at the eggs. Their broken yolks were leaking out through the cracked shells. She looked up in agony at the Turkish princess, who shrugged, pocketed the sixty dinars, flipped her lacy veil back over her face, and walked away.

"Well!" Manda announced, grinning. "That was certainly a good beginning!"

"Those," said Mama, "are the last eggs you are touching all day, my girl!" Angrily she ripped off several sheets of newspaper which she had brought along for the wrapping of eggs and vegetables. "Clean up that mess or the flies will be swarming all over and we'll have no more sales!"

Near tears, Yanya wrapped the boxful of leaking eggs in the newspaper.

"Take it to the park," said Manda sympathetically. (They were not, after all, *her* eggs.) "Put it under some bushes."

Yanya did as the widow suggested. When she'd hidden the mess of broken eggs she looked around for the water. Her mother had said there was drinking water in the park. Then she saw it, a skinny pipe sticking out of the ground. She stooped down to drink, and pressed the button. Water spurted out brownish and warm. It tasted rusty.

As she walked slowly back to her mother she thought suddenly of the doll standing in the window, arms outstretched toward her.

"If you were mine," she whispered to the doll, "I'd name you Lula. I'd tell you all my troubles, Lula. And then maybe they wouldn't seem so bad."

When she returned to her mother's side she stood perfectly still. The best plan was to do nothing and say nothing at all. That way she could not possibly get into trouble. And maybe then Mama would bring her to the market again next week.

Yanya *did* want to come back again. Of that she was very certain.

Even though she stood stiff and silent, asking no questions at all, she saw a good deal.

By nine o'clock the market had become very crowded.

There were many Moslem women. She realized now that the first woman had not been a princess. Many others were even more beautiful, and not all wore veils. The younger ladies, particularly, wore strange-looking puffy pantaloons instead of skirts, and bright-colored, long-sleeved blouses. Some wore shawls of still another shade. But many wore only a flower or ribbon in their long, black, braided hair.

All wore scarlet lipstick, most had their long fingernails painted red. (Some who wore sandals had even painted their toenails.) And all wore sparkling necklaces which, Yanya discovered upon closer observation, were not strung with jewels but with bits of colored glass.

Despite their elegant look, however, it soon became evident that the Moslem ladies had no finer manners than did the peasant women of Bosnia or Slavonia.

Like the peasant women, they would squeeze the tomatoes, dig their nails into the potatoes. They complained about the shape of the green peppers. The carrots, they claimed, were too skinny; the cabbages did not look fresh; the eggs were much too small. Often when they were told the price, they would simply give a disdainful look, and pass on to examine someone else's produce.

Yanya noted with some surprise that her mother always treated the Moslem ladies with great deference. When a peasant woman handled one of her potatoes or made insulting remarks about her eggs, Mama would let sharp words fly. But when the Moslem ladies did the same thing, Mama only smiled and nodded as though she felt honored to have her tomatoes pinched by such pale and slender, red-nailed hands.

It was the Bosnian women Yanya liked most. They reminded her of her happy childhood in Bosnia before the family had moved. It was easy to tell them from the Slavonians, for most Bosnian women wore full-skirted, ankle-length dresses of white linen—high-necked, long-sleeved. Indeed, the older women looked as though they had merely tied a colored apron around their nightgowns to come to market.

But the younger women were beautiful, Yanya

thought. On their slender figures the white dresses seemed festive and party-like. They walked straight and tall, for since childhood they had been accustomed to carrying fruit, vegetables, and buckets of water on their heads.

It was also easy to tell the married women from the single girls. Every married woman wore her hair parted in the center, and a kerchief on her head. But the single girls wore their long hair parted on the side and generally went bareheaded.

Watching them, Yanya soon became aware that more was going on at this market than the buying and selling of food and clothing. If a young Bosnian man saw a girl he liked, he might amble over, give a tweak to her blouse, or throw a pebble against her skirt, or even whistle to catch her attention. She would pay no attention whatever. If, however, he continued his efforts, she might reward him with a word, or a smile.

And, perhaps, an hour later Yanya would see them strolling down the street hand in hand.

Yanya could also tell at a glance which of the men were from Bosnia. They wore wide trousers of white or green, blue, even red. Their wide-sleeved white linen shirts were bright with embroidered trimmings. In contrast, the Slavonians wore somber dark trousers and plain cotton shirts with the sleeves rolled up.

Presently she noticed that no Bosnian man ever

tried to approach a Slavonian girl. Curiosity over-came her vow to be silent, and she asked her mother why this should be.

It was Manda who answered. "No self-respecting Slavonian girl would think of talking to a Bosnian clod! So the Bosnians don't waste their time asking."

"*I* think the Bosnian men look very handsome," Yanya replied indignantly.

"Well, *they* will agree with you on that!" said Manda, and the conversation ended.

Yanya wondered who would throw pebbles or whistle at *her* when she was old enough.

The answer seemed all too clear: no one. If she dressed like the other girls in her town and wore a bright-flowered skirt and blouse, the Slavonian men would walk away as soon as they heard her Bosnian accent. They might even insult her as the children in Bosnjaci did now, mimicking the way she spoke.

She could, of course, dress like a Bosnian girl since she had been born in that province. But the Bosnian men would no doubt walk away as soon as they learned that she now lived in the province of Sla-vonia.

There was one way, of course, to avoid such insults. She could wear black. *No* young man was permitted to approach a single girl in mourning.

There were, Yanya noted, many women in mourn-ing. Some—like Mama—were no doubt in mourning for a dead baby. But many, she knew, had lost husbands in the war. The women in their long black dresses stood out like terrible memories moving through the color and sunshine of the marketplace.

Suddenly Yanya heard an eerie singsong sound. It came from the top of the strange, tall tower. A man was there, high on a balcony.

"Who is *that,* Mama?" Yanya exclaimed. "That man in the red hat. . . . Why is he making that terrible sound?"

"Hush!" Her mother's voice was sharp as a slap. Then she lowered her voice. "He's the *muezzin.* He's calling the Moslems to prayer. Look around."

Yanya looked. To her astonishment, she saw that all the Moslem ladies in the marketplace had turned toward the tower. With hands pressed together, they were bowing up and down, up and down. A few in the park were kneeling in the grass, heads touching the ground.

"What are they doing, Mama?" she whispered.

"Praying," said Mama.

"Why do they all face the tower?"

"It's the Moslem church," said Mama.

Yanya had many more questions about this strange way of praying, but she did not dare ask anything more. Mama had already given her more answers than she expected. Usually Mama had a single retort to any question. "Children should listen—not ask!"

Within a few minutes the muezzin had finished walking round the tower balcony, uttering his chanting cries. He disappeared. The Moslem women in the marketplace resumed their shopping. And the sounds in the square rose up as before.

"Come, girl," Mama announced, "we're going home."

"Already?"

"I've sold everything," said Mama. "We must hurry now. Your papa will be waiting for his lunch."

Manda also had sold all her wares. But she seemed in no hurry to return.

"I believe I'll just stay on a bit," she said to Mama.

As Yanya followed her mother down the street, she turned to wave at Manda and saw with some surprise that the widow had taken off her head scarf. She was bareheaded like the young single girls.

As they neared the shop window where Lula stood, Yanya pulled at her mother's skirt. "Could we stop just a minute? To look at the doll."

"Your papa will be waiting," Mama said. But she allowed Yanya to stop.

And for a long, still moment they stood close, mother and daughter, staring through the grimy glass window at the beautiful doll.

4

Of all the market sights and sounds and excitements, the one image which stuck most persistently in Yanya's mind was that of Lula.

When she went to bed that night she imagined Lula lying beside her, and she whispered private words to the doll. The next morning she awoke and turned in bed, half expecting to find Lula beside her. All through the night she had dreamed about the doll.

The baby was crying. Grumbling to herself, Yanya got out of bed and picked up Pero, who was smelly and wet. His cries changed to shrieks the moment she started to unwind his diapers.

Mama had left already. From March to November every day except market day and Sunday Mama worked in the fields for a farmer named Perović. She worked without pay, but in return for her labors Perović gave her an acre that she could farm for her family. This was great good luck, for without that acre they would have starved.

Yanya let Pero crawl about on the floor while she boiled his semolina. Then she fed him, burped him, and got breakfast for herself and for Papa.

"Girl," Papa said as he sipped at his hot coffee, "come here. I've some news for you."

Yanya returned to his bedside.

"Girl—" Papa cleared his throat loudly, as if not knowing quite how to proceed. Finally he said, "I've had a letter."

"Yes, Papa?" She waited.

Intently, he tapped with his spoon at the shell of the soft-boiled egg. "In fact," he said then, "the letter came some weeks ago."

Yanya nodded. And waited.

Suddenly, all in one long sentence, Papa announced, "My mother's coming tomorrow to stay with us; I haven't told your mother yet because she doesn't like my mother, but I want you to understand that my mother is a very fine lady and no matter what your mother says you are to be very kind to your grandmother. Do you understand?"

"Yes, Papa," Yanya said. Then she asked, "Is your mother very old?" Very old people could, she knew, be as much extra work as babies.

"Old?" Papa shouted the word on a laugh. "Old? She's not old. She's sixty-two and as lively as you are."

"Oh," said Yanya, relieved. "Well, I promise you, Papa, *I* will be very happy to see her—no matter what Mama says!"

As she went about her chores that day she felt doubly delighted. Perhaps, she kept chanting to herself, *Baka* [Grandma] will wash the breakfast dishes. (Yanya hated dishwashing, for she generally managed to burn herself when she ladeled out the water that was always kept boiling in the huge black pot on the stove.) Perhaps Baka will feed the geese. (Yanya was frightened of the geese, for they sometimes nipped her.) Perhaps Baka will clean out the rabbit cages . . . sweep the yard . . . bring cold water from the well . . . scrub the kitchen floor . . . feed the chickens . . . collect the eggs . . . make the beds . . . fix the lunch . . . prepare the dinner . . . and, especially, wash out Pero's smelly diapers.

Perhaps, indeed, this lively Baka would do *every*thing, so that Yanya could spend her time playing, and going to school like the other girls her age.

Furthermore, Baka would probably bring her a present. A grandmother coming to stay would certainly arrive with some splendid gift for a granddaughter she had never seen. A doll, perhaps. Everyone knew that girls liked dolls. Baka might even pass through the market town of Orasja on her way here to her new home in Bosnjaci. Baka might see Lula in the store window. The very thing! she would think. What a splendid present for Yanya!

That morning Yanya spent so much time dreaming of all the chores Baka would do—and the present Baka would bring—that she got very little of her own work done. At lunchtime, when Mama came home to nurse the baby, Yanya had to stand, her head bent in shame, as Mama scolded her for being such a good-for-nothing lazy girl.

When Mama left once again for the fields, Papa called, "Girl, come here!"

Yanya went into the bedroom, afraid. Would *he* shout at her, too?

But Papa was very kind. "Please, girl," he said, "try to do your best today so your mama won't be cross. After all, I want her in a good mood this evening when I break the news about Baka."

"Yes, Papa," said Yanya. That afternoon she did all her chores quickly and well. And while she was working she talked and sang songs to Lula, for by now she felt certain that the next day the doll would belong to her.

That night Yanya woke up to the sound of sharp voices. Papa, it seemed, had broken the news to

Mama, who was answering back in a manner Yanya had never heard before. Usually, when Papa gave Mama orders that she deemed unjust, she would mumble and grumble—but not so that Papa could hear. Now, however, Mama was so angry that she seemed unable to control her words. They exploded from her.

"Your mother never thought I was good enough for you. She did her best to see that you wouldn't marry me. How is it that now I am good enough for Her Majesty to come and live with?"

"She has nowhere else to go," said Papa.

"Nowhere *else?* She has seven other sons and a daughter. Let them put her up and put up with her."

"They have," said Papa.

"Aha!" Mama cried. "As I thought. They've all thrown her out!"

Papa answered by saying nothing at all.

"Well," said Mama, "I'm no more saintly than they are. She may stay for a few weeks—until she finds somewhere else to go."

"Woman!" Papa thundered. "This is *my* house. You are *my* wife. You take orders from *me*. My mother is coming. And she will stay here as long as she likes. Which may mean, as long as she lives. Do you understand?"

After a long, stiff moment of silence, Mama said in a tight voice, "She may be here. But I will act as if she's not!"

No more words were spoken after that.

Yanya lay very still. Worry sat like a hard, cold lump inside her. Perhaps the arrival of Baka would mean more trouble instead of less. But it would not matter how much trouble Baka brought with her—if she only brought Lula as well.

At noontime the next day Yanya sat by the open window, waiting. The house was clean. The beds were made—even Baka's bed. Early this morning Papa's friend, Mata Lesić, had come in to hammer some boards together for a bed. And Mata's wife had followed later, carrying the straw-stuffed mattress she had made. It seemed that Papa had arranged these matters weeks ago. It also seemed that half the village knew of Baka's arrival, but no one had dared mention the matter to Mama. She was the last to learn of it.

Now the roadway was lined with children waiting, for the arrival of any new resident was an event in Bosnjaci.

Suddenly Yanya heard distant shouting, "Hey! Baka! There she is! Yanya's baka. She's coming."

Leaning far out the window, Yanya saw Mata Lesić's horse and cart coming down the dusty dirt road. He had gone to meet Baka at the railroad station. Mata Lesić sat on the front seat. Behind sat a tall figure in black. She was waving in a queenly way to the children who ran alongside the cart or hung out of open windows to watch her.

Yanya was overcome by a mixture of shyness and excitement. After all, it was *her* baka who was arriving. She should be out there proudly leading the crowd of welcoming children. Yet she could not move from the window.

Not until the horse and cart had pulled up before the house and Baka, unaided, had jumped down to the ground did Yanya run out to meet her.

"And who is *this* big girl?" said Baka.

Yanya, swept by shyness, stared down at Baka's sheepskin slippers.

"Could you be my granddaughter Yanya?" Baka put her fingers under Yanya's chin and lifted her face.

Yanya was surprised to see that her grandmother's skin was unlined. The hair which showed beneath the kerchief was dark. Baka did not look old at all. And she was smiling.

Yanya smiled back.

They started into the house together. Then Baka said, "Wait!" She hurried back to the cart and hauled out a large red-and-black striped canvas bag.

Yanya's heart began thudding. There was a bulge in the bag—just the shape of Lula's head!

"I'll help you with that bag," Mata Lesić called out.

But Baka waved him away. "I'm used to doing for myself," she said, and marched on into the house. Yanya followed close behind.

Mama came in the back door. She took the baby from his cradle, nursed him in the kitchen, brought him back to his bed, and left, without saying a single word to Baka, to Yanya, or to Papa.

Baka seemed to take no notice of any of this. She greeted Papa, who told her that she would be sleeping in the other room.

Baka peered in. "There are three beds in there," she announced.

"Marko and Ivo will be coming home next week," Papa said. "When school starts."

"Where are they now?" asked Baka.

"Working for a farmer."

Baka nodded. "I will be glad to meet my grandsons," she said. "Though I did not expect to be sharing a room with them."

"Well," said Papa, "you'll have privacy during the day. At least the room has a door that closes."

Baka went into the room and hoisted the canvas bag onto the corner bed. Yanya followed her, watching hopefully. Then Baka smiled, reached into her apron pocket, and took out a dusty, wrinkled apple with bits of tobacco clinging to it. This she presented to Yanya as though it were a great prize.

Dutifully, Yanya mumbled, "Thank you, Baka." She stared hard at the canvas bag.

"Well!" said Baka. "I'm tired from my trip. I think I'll sleep for a little while." She took off her sheepskin slippers, placed the canvas bag at the end of her bed, and lay down, resting her feet upon it.

Yanya stood in the doorway, watching.

In a few minutes the sound of the old lady's snoring filled the room.

After a week it was all too clear that the wrinkled apple was the only gift Baka had brought.

The canvas bag, which she unpacked under Yanya's still hopeful eyes, held only a black skirt, a shawl, some underwear, and a beautiful brass set for making Turkish coffee.

Many times each day Baka would make herself cups of Turkish coffee, which she sweetened with the lump sugar she carried about in her apron pocket. Sometimes she held a rough-cut lump of sugar between her teeth, and sucked the coffee through it.

She drank her Turkish coffee at the kitchen table

or, when the weather was warm, sitting on the bench by the roadside. Then she would roll herself a cigar from the packet of paper and pouch of tobacco she also carried in her large pocket. And that is how she spent her days, sitting and sipping and smoking. She did no work whatever, except to cook her own food, make her own bed and, on occasion, wash out her own clothes.

Yanya sometimes asked her mother whether Baka might not look after the baby so that she could go out to play. But Mama's reply was always the same. "I don't want her doing anything, do you understand? She's a guest. Just leave her alone."

Since Baka spoke very little, made no trouble, and offered no help, it was almost as though she had not joined the household at all.

But as the cold weather came on, Yanya found that she and her grandmother were becoming friends. When her work was done she would sit with Baka by the small iron stove. Or sometimes Baka asked Yanya to massage her back. At such times they would talk together of private things. Baka spoke of the days when she had been young and beautiful and had a handsome lover from Herzegovina who kissed her under the apple trees. She had not been allowed to marry this young man for he had an aunt who was crazy and Baka's parents were afraid that this defect might be carried on in the family line. So Baka had settled for a Bosnian peasant who got drunk and beat her every Saturday night. Yet she had remained faithful in soul and spirit to the apple-tree lover.

Since Yanya had no romantic memories to offer, she told Baka her most private dream: that someday, somehow, she would be able to buy Lula.

Baka seemed to see no more possibility of this coming to pass than did Yanya herself. Nevertheless, she would always nod and say wisely, "If you want something enough, you can make it happen."

Since Baka was sixty-two and had seen much in life, Yanya was convinced that what her grandmother told her was true. Her chief worry was that someone else would buy Lula before she herself was able to do so.

5

Yanya was often lonely during the long winter months. She was trapped in the house because she had no shoes. When she had to go out to the back-yard toilet, she ran quickly through the snow so that her feet would not freeze. Sometimes she put on the boots her father had brought back from the war. But they were so tall she could not bend her knees. Besides, they had many holes.

In the evening she was loneliest of all, for then her work was finished and she had nothing to do.

Her older brothers, Marko and Ivo, ran out every night as soon as supper was over to be with their friends. Papa had friends who came in to play cards with him, or to talk about fishing or farming or the war. Mama had friends who came over to sit by the table beneath the old lamp on the kitchen wall, and do their needlework while they gossiped about matters which Yanya did not find interesting at all. Baka would sit in a dark corner listening to the women, never joining in, but chuckling sometimes. If Mama went out after dinner to do her needlework at someone else's home, Baka always went right to bed.

So Yanya was all alone. She would often sit by the window, staring out at the faraway stars which pricked the darkness. She would gaze at the snow-roofed cottages and the silhouettes of the young women who sat by the lighted windows, sewing. Sometimes a man stopped beneath a window and whistled. Presently the girl in the window would disappear, only to emerge out the front door, wrapped in a winter shawl. And the two would walk off, hand in hand, into the secret night.

It was then that Yanya longed for her doll the most. Lula would keep her company in the long and lonely nighttimes.

"Soon, when spring comes, I will see you again," she would whisper. "Please, Lula, wait there for me. Don't let anyone else take you away."

The winter dragged slowly by. Yanya's impatience for the coming of spring made each of the cold days seem to stretch out endlessly. Without proper shoes she could not return to the market town until the snows had melted. But Mama had shoes, so she could go to Orasja as soon as the ice had broken up on the river Sava and the ferryboat could cross once more. And Mama had promised to stop by the store window to see whether Lula was still there.

To help make the days pass more quickly, Yanya started teaching herself to read. She found Ivo's primer, and in the evenings when Mama was out she would sit by the oil lamp puzzling over the strange symbols. Sometimes Ivo helped her, though he was always busy and eager to be off doing other things. Sometimes Papa helped her, but he grew angry easily and would shout that she was stupid.

Baka could not help, for she had never learned to read or write.

And Mama would not help. "If you've all that time to spare," Mama would say crossly, "I suggest you do something worthwhile. Start on your dowry, like the other girls your age!"

But this Yanya flatly refused to do. "I won't *need* sheets and embroidered napkins! Because I don't plan to get married." She had no intention of scrubbing her life away, letting her belly get fat with one baby after another, some of whom lived, some of whom died. "Instead of all that," Yanya would say, "I'm going to see the wide world!"

Baka had once met some sailors in the Yugoslav merchant marine who told her about the places they had seen—New York City, Africa, Japan. Time had blurred the details in Baka's mind, but since Yanya showed such interest the old lady tried to weave together stories from scattered shreds of memory.

Yanya had no idea how she would ever get to such wondrous places, any more than she knew how she would one day buy Lula. She was certain only that if she hoped hard enough these things would happen.

One day in early March, Pishta the Newsman came through the streets, banging his drum and shouting loudly that the boat was running once again across the Sava.

Mama did not want to go to the market town, not yet. The road, she insisted, would be dangerous and difficult, slippery with ice and mud. Besides, there were as yet no vegetables to sell. But Yanya pleaded and begged so hard that Mama relented. The following Thursday, market day, she set off alone with her baskets. One was piled with eggs. The other held five squawking chickens, feet tied together, heads protruding from the covering cloth.

All that day Yanya went about praying: "Dear God, please let Lula still be there in the store window!" And while she prayed she fairly flew about the house doing her work. She was through by noontime. Pero, fortunately, was asleep in his crib. So she put on her father's high black boots and staggering, stumbling, she ran along the road to the edge of town. There she waited for Mama.

The sun inched slowly through clouds and across

the afternoon sky. One o'clock . . . two . . . three. Others returned from market. But not Mama.

Pero would be awake by now and screaming. Papa would be shouting for his lunch. But even though she was quaking with cold, Yanya could not move. She had to know—the first second possible—about Lula.

Finally, Mama's small figure came into view down the distant road.

Yanya ran to meet her. Several times she slid on the ice-slick road and fell. When she reached her mother Yanya went suddenly numb with terror.

Mama was scowling.

"What happened?" Yanya whispered.

"What happened!" Mama exclaimed. "I fell down twenty times on the ice. That's what happened! I'm black and blue all over. What a fool I was to go to market for the sake of a stupid child."

"But Lula— What happened to Lula? Is she still there?"

Mama nodded. "She's there all right. I even went into the shop to ask how much she cost. Seven thousand dinars! There's one thing you can be certain of, girl. She's there—and she'll stay there. No one is going to spend seven thousand dinars on a doll."

Yanya felt such relief surge through her that suddenly, unexpectedly, she started to cry.

Lula was still there . . . waiting!

Spring came early that year. The first fuzz of green appeared amid the treetops by mid-March. The apple trees were beginning to blossom. And the women of Bosnjaci were out with their brooms, sweeping the last of the caked snow and ice off the dirt roadways of town.

It was also warm enough to walk barefoot for many miles, so Yanya went again with her mother to market.

Mama was understanding. She allowed Yanya to stand for almost ten minutes staring through the dusty window glass at Lula.

"You remember me, don't you, Lula darling?" Yanya whispered.

The doll stood, stretching out her arms and smiling a little, as if longing to be held.

On the way back from the market Yanya told Lula, "Wait there for me. Don't let anyone take you away, Lula. I'll see you again next Thursday. I promise."

Every Thursday all through the spring and summer and early September Yanya stopped to see her doll.

And in between the Thursdays she dreamed of Lula, and pretended the doll was with her.

At home the stable was empty, for the cowherd came early every morning to take Rumenka, their skinny old cow, out to pasture. So Yanya built a private place for Lula in a dusky, quiet corner. She made a bed of straw and hemmed a coverlet for it.

She found some pieces of wood in the toolshed, and with a saw, hammer, and nails fashioned a small table, a chair, and a chest to hold Lula's red silk dress, her petticoats, and shoes and socks when she undressed her doll for the night. She also made Lula a nightgown, cut from a piece of Pero's new diaper.

Yanya would sit in the stable and talk to Lula. She sang to the doll, told her stories, and also at times revealed her most secret thoughts. She confessed, for example, her very mixed feelings about starting school in the fall.

She was excited; she wanted to learn. And she wanted also to escape the daily drudgery of housework. But she was, at the same time, scared.

The town children often teased her because of her Bosnian accent. But at least now, when they gathered around her, taunting and jeering, she could run home. In school she would be trapped, with nowhere to run, nowhere to hide.

The children teased her also because of the clothes she wore. She had no fancy white petticoats or carefully embroidered aprons or blouses with shirring at the sleeves like the other girls in Bosnjaci. She had only one simple skirt and blouse and, because she was growing fast, both were now too small.

The night before the first day of school Yanya filled the heavy iron with glowing red coals from the fire and pressed her skirt and blouse.

Early the next morning, feeling pale with fear, she set off for school with her oldest brother, Marko. This year Ivo would go to the afternoon session—because of the shoes. When the cold weather came, Yanya could wear Ivo's shoes—with extra socks and rags stuffed inside them. When she returned at lunchtime, Ivo would set off in the shoes.

As she trudged along beside her big brother, Yanya wished that Ivo was the one taking her to school the first day. Ivo sometimes stood up for her. When the children mocked her he would often shout back at them. At times he had even chased them off with a stick. But Marko, who was fifteen and in his final year at school, regarded such matters as too childish to warrant his attention. He was interested in one thing only: soccer. As they neared the schoolhouse, Marko saw two boys from his team and ran off to catch up with them.

Yanya walked on, very slowly.

She had often passed the school before—when she took corn to the mill, bought Turkish coffee for Baka at the shop, or went to church.

But now the school looked bigger than ever. It stretched three stories high, the tallest building in town. The curtainless windows stared out like many dark eyes looking down at her.

Children were crowding in through the doorway, chattering, laughing. Everyone seemed to have friends to talk to. Yanya had never felt so small, so alone, in all her life.

"Oh, Lula," she whispered, "how I wish you were coming to school with me today!"

6

Yanya mounted the stone steps and entered the high front door of the school. Swarms of children of all sizes were running through the corridor, which seemed about to burst with the sound of shouting voices. She had never before realized there were so many children in the town of Bosnjaci.

So many children, but no one she knew.

She took the carefully folded registration slip from her pocket. Once again she unfolded it and read the words—YANYA MARCOVIĆ. FIRST GRADE. ROOM I. SECOND FLOOR. (MORNING SESSION : 8 TO 12.)

She knew the directions, of course, as if they were stamped into her brain. But it made her feel less awkward to stand consulting the registration slip that Mama had brought home for her three days ago.

Mama, Yanya suspected, would never have registered her at all if Papa had not received three official notices from the Town Hall. The final notice had been short and sharp. It said that, according to the ruling of the new communist government of Yugoslavia, Papa would have to pay a large fine if Yanya was not registered at once. Papa had therefore shouted at Mama, ordering her to go that very day to sign up Yanya for school. Mama had gone, slamming the front door hard behind her. Several hours later she reappeared with the white paper, which she handed to Yanya without a word.

"I'm sorry, Mama," Yanya had said, feeling very guilty. "It's not my idea to go to school. It's the law."

"Law!" Mama exploded. "Is the law going to send someone here to help me with the housework while you're at school? Is the law going to work my fields for me? For what does a girl need an education? She gets married. She sews, she cooks, she cleans, she looks after the children. You already know how to do all those things. You already have all the education you'll need in life."

"Yes, Mama," Yanya had replied meekly, judging that now was not the best time to announce that she did not intend to spend her life washing and cooking and sewing.

She climbed the broad wooden stairway, holding

the bannister so that she would not be knocked over by the children racing up and down. When she entered Room I on the second floor the shouts and screams were louder than ever. The window ledge was crowded with first-graders leaning out, waving and hollering at friends, brothers, and sisters in the yard below. Others were standing on the benches or sitting on the desks, shouting, waving their arms. Still others were scrawling large chalk pictures on the blackboard.

Yanya sat down at a desk in the front row so that she would be in a good position to see and hear well, ready to start learning when the teacher arrived.

Presently Comrade Lesić strode through the door, a tall and handsome black-haired man with a small dark mustache. He was dressed as other men in town dressed when they went to church or to a wedding. He wore a dark-blue suit, a shirt, a tie, and shiny black shoes. He walked to his desk.

"QUIET!" he bellowed.

The children looked at him, startled.

"Everyone sit down," said Comrade Lesić, the words dropping like shots into the sudden silence.

The children sat.

"Welcome to the first grade," said Comrade Lesić, shaping his mouth into a stiff smile below the small mustache.

The children made no answer.

"Since this is the first day any of you have ever

been in a schoolroom," said the teacher, "I will excuse your bad behavior—THIS ONE TIME!" The words shook with threat. "In the future, when you enter the room, I want you to take your seats. When I come in, you must stand until I say, 'Be seated, children.' " He took a piece of paper from his desk. "Now," he announced, "I will call the roll. When I say your name stand and announce, 'I am here.' "

The smaller children were assigned seats in the front row; the tallest were sent to desks at the back. Since Yanya was older than the other children, she was one of the tallest in the class. The teacher moved her to a bench at the back where four students shared the long desk.

Comrade Lesić then gave out instructions about the schedule, what to do when the school bell rang, what books they would need to buy. He concluded with the announcement that each child should come the next day with a slate and chalk. Then he dismissed the class.

The first day of school had lasted only half an hour. Yanya went home and did all the housework she had thought she would never have to do again.

The second day Comrade Lesić started off by drawing a row of short leaning lines on the blackboard. He asked the children to copy these lines on their slates. Then to erase the lines.

Each slate came with a small erasing sponge set

into a hole in the wooden frame. But Yanya had borrowed Ivo's slate. He had lost the sponge. She was the only one in the class who had to erase with spit and a piece of old rag.

Then Comrade Lesić drew on the blackboard some lines which leaned the other way. These, too, the children copied. For one hour they drew leaning lines, erased, drew more leaning lines. This, the teacher then announced, was the start of learning how to write letters.

Yanya soon became bored with the leaning lines. Since she already knew how to write all the letters, she filled her slate up with the alphabet, hoping that she might not have to make lines any more. Then she waited for the teacher, who was walking slowly from desk to desk, viewing the work of each child. While she waited she began to write all the words she knew—CAT, DOG, HOUSE—and the name of every member of her family, including Rumenka the cow.

When Comrade Lesić finally came to look at her slate, he whistled in surprise, asked Yanya how old she was and where she had learned her letters. When he discovered that she also knew how to read, he sent her off with a note to Comrade Jurić in the room across the hall. Yanya had been promoted to the second grade.

Comrade Jurić was a tall, plain, skinny woman who always wore tight sweaters. She also had bad breath, and she seemed to be short-sighted for she would lean over very close to each child as she walked by the rows of desks to inspect the work. Whenever Yanya saw Comrade Jurić coming toward her she would take a deep breath which she held until the teacher said, as she always did, "Excellent." Then Yanya let her breath out slowly as the teacher passed on.

She was relieved when, after two weeks, Comrade Jurić decided that Yanya should be promoted to the third grade. She was relieved, that is, until she sat in the front row of Comrade Marsić's class. This teacher was very short, very fat, and very mean. He carried a ruler in his belt like a sword and he was forever whipping it out in order to hit some student over the knuckles or on the head. This was invariably accompanied by Comrade Marsić's shouts. He also had a silent punishment. He had spread a patch of corn kernels in the corner of the classroom, and the offender would be sent to kneel there for an hour. Should the student begin to cry with pain or otherwise make a sound, he would also receive a crack on the head with Comrade Marsić's ruler.

Yanya hated the third grade. The work was interesting. They studied geography, history, biology, and fractions—subjects she had never known existed. But she was terrified of Comrade Marsić's slashing ruler. She was also afraid of her classmates. She was the youngest and smallest child in the third grade. Furthermore, she was the only new girl in the

class. There was also the problem of her Bosnian
accent.

In the second grade Comrade Jurić, who was kind
despite her smelly breath, had explained again and

again to the class that they must not laugh at Yanya when she spoke. Actually, Comrade Jurić told them, the Bosnian accent was pure; the Slavonian accent was not. "If anything," said Comrade Jurić, "it is Yanya who should be laughing at *you*. She speaks perfect Croatian."

This had helped in Comrade Jurić's class. But Comrade Marsić—who spoke with a strong Slavonian dialect—had made no mention of Yanya's pure accent. Nor did he make the slightest attempt to stop the children when they teased her. Which they did, at every opportunity.

The worst time of all was recess when the class went down into the asphalt yard to play. In other grades the boys played volleyball and basketball at recess time. The girls played jump rope and hopscotch and tag. And often the boys and girls joined together to do folk dancing.

But in the third grade the favorite recess sport seemed to be gathering around Yanya to push and shove her from one to the other while they chanted:

> *Yanya, Yanya, born in Bosnia,*
> *Dressed like a beggar,*
> *Speaks like a freak!*

During these sessions Yanya tried her best not to cry. Nevertheless, by the time recess was over she usually returned to the classroom with tears streaming down her face. Finally she told Comrade Marsić that she had hurt her leg, and asked permission to remain in the empty classroom during recess time. Comrade Marsić merely shrugged. "If you wish," he said.

After that things were a little better. When the children had dashed out, and Comrade Marsić had stalked off to the teachers' room, Yanya would sit in the sudden quiet of the classroom doing her homework. She was grateful for this period, because at home Mama never allowed her any time for homework. Mama scolded Ivo and Marko when they tried to escape without doing their homework. But Yanya was put to work cooking, cleaning, and caring for Pero as soon as she returned from school. In order to get any homework done she had to hide in the outhouse.

Because Yanya could now do her homework in school, and because the children had less time to tease her, life became more pleasant. And she found herself dreaming more and more about Lula. When her days had been blackest, thoughts of the doll had only hurt. Lula was just one more reminder of the joys of life that could never come to pass—for Yanya. But when she realized that things were, in fact, becoming brighter, it again began to seem possible that she might one day own the doll.

In fact, she set about thinking of ways to make this come to pass.

7

Mama's birthday was coming. Yanya decided that
if she bought Mama a splendid present, Mama might
respond by buying Lula when Yanya's birthday came
around. The only trouble was, of course, that Yanya
had no money with which to buy Mama a present.

Then an idea hit her. Their home was not far from
the town cemetery. She had noticed that people sometimes brought beautiful flowers to leave by the
graves. Not wild flowers. These were garden-grown
and fashioned into wreaths or fancy bouquets tied
with wide, shiny ribbon. Sunday seemed to be ceme-

tery day, for it was then that most people came to visit the graves. They departed by evening, leaving the fancy flowers behind to wither and die, unnoticed.

Mama's birthday fell, fortunately, on a Sunday.

After supper that Sunday evening Yanya took her composition book to the cemetery and sat, leaning back against a tall, cracked gravestone, copying out sentences in her most careful handwriting, waiting for it to grow dark. At times, when someone passed with an especially beautiful bouquet, she would peep out to see exactly where it had been left.

Unfortunately, several families stayed on and on. Children played hide-and-seek among the gravestones, their shrill cries piercing the quietness. Would they never go home?

She finished her composition and then, to help pass the time, she started practicing her Slavonian dialect. She was determined to lose her Bosnian accent so that she would sound exactly the same as the other children in town.

Arms of darkness stretched in lengthening shadows that seemed to reach out at her like monster fingers. Every instinct made her want to run from the eerie graveyard. But she sat there, perhaps because she was too terrified to move. The October afternoon had been warm, but as night came on, the air turned chilly. She had brought her black woolen shawl and she huddled in it, holding it tight around her body. Still, she started to shiver.

Finally, the graveyard emptied. As darkness settled, and the crickets and frogs sounded out in their nighttime chorus, Juro the Cemetery Man rang the bell in the small chapel and called out in a loud voice: "Everybody leave, please. The cemetery is now closed."

As soon as Juro had gone, clanking the iron gate behind him, Yanya darted out from her hiding place.

Stooping low, she ran to a nearby grave where a lovely bunch of white chrysanthemums had been left during the afternoon.

Holding the flowers carefully beneath her shawl, she raced for the low, stone cemetery wall, climbed over it and ran, terrified, down the dirt road, through the darkness, until she reached home.

She waited then, squatting by the front door until she had regained her breath, and until she stopped shaking. Then she stood up, smoothed her hair, took the flowers from beneath her shawl, and went inside.

Mama was nursing the baby; she hummed softly, her eyes closed. She often sat like this when she nursed Pero in the nighttime. The baby was now eighteen months of age, and Yanya felt he was far too old for such close attentions.

"Mama," Yanya said. Then, since her mother still sat, eyes closed and humming, she repeated in a louder voice, "Mama! Happy Birthday!"

She smiled, and held out the bunch of flowers, making sure that the beautiful broad white ribbon was in full view.

Mama opened her eyes. She gasped.

"For you, Mama, dear," Yanya said. "A present for your birthday. A *present*." She said the word twice to make sure that Mama understood.

"Where did you get those flowers?" Mama asked in a faint voice.

"I . . . got them, Mama. For you."

"Where did they come from?"

"They're flowers for your birthday, Mama."

"They're from the *dead!*" Abruptly Mama put little Pero on the floor. He started to scream.

Mama stood up. "Admit it!" she shouted at Yanya. "You *stole* those flowers. Stole them from the dead."

Yanya said nothing at all. Her eyes filled with tears.

Suddenly a voice came from the corner. Baka was sitting there in the shadows. "Don't scold the child," Baka said sternly. "She meant well."

Mama turned on Baka. "Mind your own business, old lady! Do you think I want to bring up a thief?" She turned back to Yanya. "Girl, you march right out of here with those death flowers and take them straight back where they came from!"

"Mama!" It had been bad enough waiting in the darkness of the graveyard to collect the flowers. But at least there had been people about most of the time. To return there now—all alone!

"You're not going to send that child out again!" Baka stood up and stalked out of the corner shadows. "If you don't want the flowers, throw them away. No one will know the difference."

"The dead will know!" Mama shrieked. "Whose grave did you steal them from, heh?" She turned once again on Yanya. "Whoever it was, do you want them to rise up and come here to take back their flowers?"

Numb with fright, Yanya shook her head.

"Then get out! Get out of here with those flowers of death!"

"Wait!" Baka said. She took her shawl from the peg by the door. "If she goes, I will go with her!" Then she said gently to Yanya, "Come, little one. The ghosts won't rise if we go together."

The moon slid up from behind the distant trees as they started down the road, hand in hand. The pale light cast grotesque shadows. But Yanya was no longer frightened. She felt closer to her grandmother than she had ever felt to any human being. But she could not tell Baka how grateful she was, for her throat was clogged tight with tears.

8

By the first of March Papa was feeling better. In fact, he was strong enough to go to work again. His brother Stefan gave him a job at the mill.

It was because of Stefan that Yanya's mother had come to Bosnjaci during the war when their cottage in Bosnia was burned to the ground. Yanya remembered well the night they arrived at Stefan's house, after riding three days and nights in a cattle car crowded with soldiers and with other families fleeing from disaster. They were a sorry-looking lot: Mama, her body swollen with the baby who had turned out to be Pero. The two boys, Ivo and Marko, so dirty that their faces were black and their clothing smelled. The yellow cow, Rumenka. And Yanya. Papa was not with them. He had already been taken prisoner by the Germans.

Since Papa had rarely written to his brother, Stefan did not even know the name of Papa's wife. Yet, when they knocked on the door late at night, Stefan had taken them in. He ordered his wife to get out of bed and make them a hot meal. Then Stefan had let them sleep in his barn, where they remained until Mama finally saved enough money to buy the small house in which they lived now.

Stefan was kind. But his wife, Bosiljka, was not. She regarded Mama as a peasant because Mama worked in the fields.

Bosiljka, on the other hand, thought of herself as a lady. She was the Miller's Daughter. She constantly reminded Stefan that he owed his high position in town to the fact that she had consented to marry him. Otherwise, he would be a mere farmer slaving away under the hot sun like everyone else.

Bosiljka had forbidden her own children to have anything to do with their cousins who lived in the barn. And when Yanya's mother had finally moved her family to the little house on the edge of town, Bosiljka had also forbidden her husband to visit them. After Papa returned from the prison camp, Stefan had come several times to see his brother. But then Bosiljka heard about these secret visits, and Stefan came no more.

Now, however, he had helped them again. Papa was not yet well enough to work in the fields. So Stefan gave him a job keeping accounts at the mill.

Papa worked at the mill every day from six in the morning until five in the evening, six days a week. Yanya longed to visit him, to see his office. But since she went to school six days a week from eight until twelve, and had to come home then to take care of Pero and do the housework, there seemed to be no time left over to walk the two miles to the mill and back.

One bright blue Saturday afternoon, however, spring came in so warm and blossom-scented that she announced to Baka she was taking Pero for a walk on this beautiful day. And she set off with him for the mill.

At first Pero was fine, running here and there, picking roadside flowers, throwing stones at butterflies. But soon he grew tired, started to cry, and wanted to return home.

"We *must* see Papa," Yanya told him sternly. "For a very important reason!" (Perhaps by the time they reached the mill she would think up what this reason could be.)

She held Pero's hand and half pulled him. But finally he cried so hard that she picked him up and staggered along, carrying him as far as she could. Then they would sit down and rest. After which Pero would walk a bit farther. And finally, after two long hours of sitting, carrying, walking, scolding, they reached the mill.

It was a wide, flat-roofed brick building with many small windows. She had visited it often when they lived in Uncle Stefan's barn. On the first floor there were great machines with many wheels, to grind the corn and wheat and maize. On the second floor was a series of large wooden pipes leading up from the grinding machines below. Under each pipe was a wooden trough: one for rye flour; one for wheat flour; one for corn meal; one for maize. Uncle Stefan worked here. He wore a white baker's hat and his face was always pale from the flour dust.

Papa, she knew, had his office on the first floor by the large backyard where the carts drew up to bring their grain to be ground at the mill. She and Pero made their way amid the carts and the horses which stomped impatiently and flicked their tails in the late afternoon sunshine. There was a wooden ramp. They walked up it. And suddenly, there was Papa seated at a desk with a strange, bright, pear-shaped thing hanging on a rope above his head.

Yanya had expected Papa to look like Uncle Stefan with his white cap and lightly floured face. Instead, Papa looked just the opposite, with a black cap and black face.

"Hello, Papa!" she exclaimed, walking up to his table. "How did you get so dirty?"

When Papa had recovered from his surprise at the sudden appearance of his two youngest children, he explained that part of his job was stoking the coal furnace. *"But . . . "* Papa said, "most of my work is bookkeeping. A very responsible position."

"What's that, Papa?" said little Pero, pointing at the bright glass pear that hung above the table.

"An electric light," said Papa.

"What's an electric light?" said Yanya. "A kind of candle?"

Papa laughed. Then he nodded. "You might call it a kind of candle." He bent and lifted her up on the table. "I'll tell you what, girl, if you can blow out this kind of candle, I'll buy you that doll for your birthday."

Yanya stared at her father. Her eyes filled with tears.

We must see Papa, she had told Pero. *For a very important reason.* She had not known then what the reason was. She had only *felt* its importance. But now she knew. Lula. Her darling, precious Lula. At last, at last after all these months and months of longing—the doll would be hers!

"Thank you, Papa," she whispered softly. Then she took a big breath. And blew at the kind of candle.

Nothing happened.

She took another breath. A bigger breath. Put her mouth very close to the bright-shaped pear. And blew again. Much harder.

Nothing happened.

"Hey, Antun," Papa called to a sooty-faced man

with a shovel who was passing by. "Come watch my little girl blow out the electric light!"

Yanya took a still bigger breath. This time surely she would blow out the light. Lula was there waiting for her in the shop window, her arms outstretched.

With one tremendous blow Yanya let out all the air inside her. The electric light burned on just as brightly as before. Papa and his friend let out shouts of laughter. And Yanya burst into tears.

"There," Papa said, taking her suddenly into his arms. "There, little one, I meant only to teach you a lesson. Some things in life are impossible, so there's no use longing after them. Whether it's blowing out an electric light or wanting a doll that costs seven thousand dinars."

Yanya said nothing to her father. She climbed down from the table and for the rest of the afternoon she sat in the corner with Pero, who had fallen asleep.

Antun gave them a ride halfway home in his cart. He kept laughing and teasing Yanya about the electric light until Papa said suddenly, "Be quiet, man!"

So Antun said nothing more.

And they all rode on in silence into the deepening evening.

After that, Yanya tried very hard not to think any more about Lula. She still dreamed about the doll in the nighttime. Sometimes she was inside the shop, taking Lula from the window, then running with her down a narrow street. But the shopkeeper, a tall, terrible man, always came after her, brandishing a sword and shouting, "Thief! Thief! She has stolen my doll!"

Sometimes the dreams were quiet and beautiful. She was walking through a field of flowers with Lula and the sun was shining. Or sometimes she was simply staring at the doll through the dusty shop window.

She could not help the nighttime dreaming. But she did try her best to turn her daytime thoughts away whenever they fastened on the doll.

By the time her birthday came at the end of March, she had convinced herself that if she got any present at all it would not be Lula.

And she was right. Her birthday present was the promise of a pair of shoes for the following winter.

"You see," said Mama, "I have the money right here. Papa has saved it from his wages. There's no sense buying the shoes now with the summer coming. You'd only outgrow them by the time it turns cold. But we'll save this money, I promise you, Yanya. No matter what, you'll have your own pair of shoes."

"Thank you very much, Mama," Yanya said. "And thank you too, Papa." She stretched her mouth into a smile and tried to look very pleased.

Springtime came and went. School ended. On the first Thursday of vacation, Mama asked Yanya to come to market with her.

Yanya surprised herself by answering with a loud "No!"

"Why on earth not?" said Mama. "I thought you loved going to market."

She did. It was true. Still, for some reason, when Thursday came, she refused to accompany Mama.

The following Thursday Mama invited her again. When Yanya once again refused, Mama said, "I *want* you to come. I may need you."

"Why?" said Yanya suddenly. "Because you're afraid you might have the baby right on the road?"

Mama's face went white. Then she turned very red. "Whatever are you talking about?" she said. "What baby? I don't know anything about any baby."

"You're getting fatter and fatter in front," Yanya announced. "You always get fat in front before a baby comes."

"Who told you such rubbish?" said Mama severely. "The stork brings a baby. You know that. I've explained it to you often enough!"

"When a stork brings me my Lula," said Yanya, "then I'll believe a stork can bring babies too!"

The following Thursday Mama was too sick to go to market. She lay in bed, groaning. Since the carrots had been picked and would spoil if they were not sold, Mama told Yanya that she would have to go to market with Manda. This time there seemed no room for argument. So, at six o'clock in the morning Yanya set off, carrying a basket of carrots in one hand, a basket of eggs in the other. And she found that sparks of excitement were shooting through her at the thought of going again to Orasja.

This spring she had carefully refrained from asking Mama whether the doll was still there in the store window. Since Mama had not mentioned seeing Lula, Yanya thought it best to assume that by this time the doll had been sold. Still, she *might* just be there waiting. It was possible. Anything, as Baka sometimes said, was possible.

Manda made a pleasant roadside companion. She laughed a good deal, especially when farmers drove by in their carts on the way to the fields. She seemed to know all of the men by name. And the men certainly seemed to know Manda.

When there was no one on the road to talk to, Manda sang. She had a strong, clear voice.

"Do you like Russian folk songs?" she said to Yanya. "A Russian priest taught me some. Ahhh," she sighed, "my beautiful priest." And she launched then into a gay, rhythmic song that made it easier to walk along quickly.

When she grew tired of singing, Manda held

cheerful conversations with Yanya. Conversations about clothes and food and goings-on at the marketplace. She spoke as though Yanya were a grown woman instead of a girl. As they walked along, chattering and laughing, Yanya began to feel she had suddenly turned into the beautiful seventeen-year-old Lisa who lived across the road.

As they neared the market town, however, Yanya fell silent. There was a strange, dry nervousness inside her.

At the Sava River the boat was waiting. She had prayed it would be on the other side. She needed more time to prepare herself.

What would she do—whatever would she do—if Lula was gone from the shop window?

She realized now that, however hard she had tried to put Lula out of her mind, she had not succeeded. Her hopes and her dreams were still centered around the beautiful doll with the small smile and the outstretched arms.

9

They had come upon it too quickly!

Lula's shop window.

Yanya was not at all prepared. Pretending she was fascinated by something on the opposite side of the street, she turned her head away from the shop window as they walked by.

Lula! Are you there? Please, my little darling, be there. Wait for me!

But she did not dare to look.

Her heart did not stop pounding until she stood beside Manda on the market square and sorted out her carrots carefully on a piece of newspaper.

For a while no buyers came, though Manda called out cheerily and joked with the passers-by. Many men stopped to talk to her. But her loud voice and laughter seemed to drive the women away. And it was the women in the marketplace who bought vegetables and eggs.

Manda did not seem very worried by the lack of customers. Several times along the road she had exclaimed, "You know, I'm just as glad your Mama didn't come along this morning!" Yanya had taken these words as a great compliment. But now she knew better. It was merely that the widow had to be a bit more constrained with Mama along. Now, however, there was nothing to hold her back. Manda had already taken off her kerchief. Her hair was long and loose, worn with a side part in the manner of the young unmarried girls.

Yanya noticed that buyers were stopping at other booths. The market was becoming more crowded. But still no women came to ask the price of Yanya's carrots and eggs. She wished she could move away from Manda. Perhaps people thought she belonged to this loud-voiced, laughing woman.

Finally a Moslem woman stopped, pointed at Yanya's carrots and asked the price.

Yanya was so startled that she stammered, "I . . .

what, madame? . . . Oh. Two dinars."

And before she quite knew what was happening, the Moslem lady had bought up all her carrots and signaled two little boys who followed her to carry them off home.

Yanya glanced up at the widow to see if she had noticed. Luckily Manda was chattering to a young man who stood smoking a cigarette and looking her over lazily as though she were a cow he was thinking of buying.

Anyone, Yanya knew, could get rid of carrots in a moment by selling them for two dinars a bunch. She had *meant* to say two dinars a carrot!

When another Moslem lady stopped to ask the price of Yanya's eggs, she answered firmly, "Three dinars apiece, madame." This was the price Mama always started at, when asked.

But the Moslem lady merely stared at Yanya as though she had not heard correctly. "*Three* dinars?" she said in a shrill voice, and stalked away on her high-heeled shoes. She had not even bothered to bargain.

Perhaps women felt it beneath them to haggle over prices with a child.

When the next customer stopped—a Bosnian peasant girl this time—Yanya promptly announced, "The eggs are two dinars apiece. For the big ones, that is. The smaller ones you may have for less."

The Bosnian girl merely laughed. "I didn't come

here to buy eggs. Only to ask if there was any drinking water about."

Yanya pointed to the park behind. "There's a pipe sticking out of the ground. If you press a button water shoots out."

The Bosnian girl thanked her and hurried off to the water fountain. Then, for what seemed an interminable time, no one stopped by to ask the price of Yanya's eggs.

Finally, the Moslem lady who had bought the carrots returned. She took some coins from the pocket of her pantaloons and held them out toward Yanya. "Since your carrots were two dinars a bunch," she said in a sweet, soft voice, "I believe this would be a fair price for your basket of eggs."

"No, madame!" Yanya said stoutly.

The Moslem lady lifted her veil. Then she lifted her eyebrows in surprise. "No?" she repeated. "Why not?"

"My eggs are worth more than my carrots," said Yanya.

The Moslem lady laughed, a tinkly, mocking sound. "Why, mala?" she said. "Are your eggs made of gold? Are they filled with gems? What sort of egg is worth more than a fresh bunch of carrots?"

Yanya felt herself flush with shame. She glanced at the widow for help. But Manda was now busy chattering to a sunburned man with a blond mustache.

"All right, then, mala," the Moslem lady said, "if your eggs are truly so valuable, I will *double* my price." She took more coins from her pocket and held out the handful toward Yanya.

The money glinted brightly in the morning sunshine. The Moslem lady now seemed to be offering her many coins. How many Yanya did not know. But perhaps if she turned down this sale, no one else would come along. And how could she return home with a basket of eggs—unsold?

She nodded. The Moslem lady let the shimmering waterfall of coins slide through her fingers into Yanya's outstretched hands. Then, carefully, she placed each egg in her market basket. She smiled at Yanya, lowered her veil, and hurried away.

When the sunburned man sauntered off, Manda looked down at her. "What?" she exclaimed. "Have you sold everything already?"

Yanya nodded. "Are we going home now?"

"*Home?*" said Manda. "Certainly *not!* The day has just started. If you've sold all your things, why don't you visit the shops? See the town?"

"Oh!" said Yanya. "*May* I?"

Manda laughed. "I know your Mama never lets you stray a foot out of her sight. But I'm not your Mama, am I? Besides, you're a big girl now. Just be sure to be back here by noontime, after the muezzin chants from his perch up there." And she pointed to the tall minaret.

Yanya did not wait, in case the widow might change her mind. She shot off like a streak.

She ran across the park, past the old people sitting out on benches like wood-carved figures under the chestnut trees. She made her way through the shoppers clustered on the brick-paved street on the other side of the park. And then she reached a row of shops she had never seen before—a wonderland behind a row of dusty plate-glass windows.

The Confectioner's Shop. Why had Mama never brought her here? There were two large trays in the window, one piled high with baklava, the other with halva. She had tasted both, for Lisa's young man sometimes brought sweets, which Lisa had on occasion let Yanya sample. Now as she stared in the window her mouth watered. She moved to the open door. Inside, behind a wooden table, stood a handsome, dark-skinned man wearing a red shirt and an apron. A gypsy. He was spooning out pink and white and chocolate ices into paper cups. The shop was crowded with children, and grownups too, chattering and laughing as they waited to buy ices.

Yanya went inside.

"How much does one of those cost?" she asked a small red-headed boy who stood licking a long frozen ice on a stick. He answered with a pure Bosnian accent, which made him seem like a sudden friend. "Five dinars," he said. "Very good, too."

Well, why not? She had money. Not much, of course. But, since there was so little, she would not be in any more disgrace if she went home with five dinars less.

She stood in line, bought herself a chocolate ice on a stick, and went outside licking slowly at the cold sweetness. She felt guilty, yet delighted. It would be this way when she was out in the wide world. She would have her own money. She could buy what she wanted. She could go where she wished.

Perhaps she would go off on her own right now! Get a job—in a confectioner's shop! Then, when she had made enough money, she would come back here to Orasja and buy Lula. If only the doll would wait for her in the shop window. Maybe if she gave the shopkeeper all the money she had right now he would promise to keep Lula for a year—until she returned with the rest of the seven thousand dinars.

Then the thought she had been trying to ignore all morning chilled through her. What if the doll were already gone?

Lula's shop was only ten minutes away. It would be easy enough to go there. Then this terrible question would be settled—one way or the other.

But she was afraid. At least now she had these hours of sudden freedom. Why risk spoiling it all with the knowledge that Lula had been sold?

The first thing to do was to count the money the Moslem woman had given her. Perhaps, after all, it *was* a great deal. Enough to buy Lula right now—with enough left over for running away.

She finished the last of the chocolate ice, then ran into the park and squatted down by the wooden fence under a lime tree. There she untied the white scarf in which she carried the money. The aluminum coins glinted in the sunlight, which fell in dappled patterns through the lime leaves high above. There were many coins. She closed her eyes and let them run through her fingers as the Moslem woman had done. If only each coin were a ten-dinar piece, a twenty-dinar piece. But she knew, even with her eyes closed, that the coins were small in size. All she had was a large pile of small coins: each one worth only one dinar or, at the very most, five.

She opened her eyes, startled by a footstep. A Bosnian peasant woman was stooping down beside her.

Quickly Yanya covered her coins.

The woman laughed. "I'm not going to steal your money, mala. I'm gathering lime leaves for tea."

Nevertheless, Yanya scooped up her coins in the kerchief and ran away. Better to find some quiet place to count her money.

The market was held on only two sides of the square. Directly across the park was the entrance to a side street that seemed deserted.

She ran out the wooden gate, past the apothecary shop . . . the barber shop . . . the furniture shop . . . the cobbler's . . . the textile shop . . . the seed shop . . . past several fine two-story homes with ornately carved wooden fences. And then into the empty side street.

There were no people here at all. The road was no longer brick, but dirt. And the buildings that lined it were hulking, unpainted structures with no windows at all. The wide door to one of them was open. She walked up slowly, cautiously; peered inside. It was a storehouse, piled high with burlap sacks of grain.

Here was the perfect private place for counting up her money.

She sat on a bench just inside the doorway, untied the white scarf that Mama had made from Ivo's old ripped shirt, and spread it out on her lap. Then, carefully, she counted the coins.

Fifty-two! That was all. Each of the shiny coins was only a one- or a two-dinar piece. The Moslem lady must have gone home to gather up all her smallest change so that she could pour the coins into Yanya's hands, making it seem like an abundance.

Next Yanya counted, and recounted, the crumpled paper money that the Moslem lady had given her for the carrots. Fifty dinars. That was all.

The total: one hundred and two.

A sick feeling went through her. Even on a bad day Mama returned home from the market with at least seven hundred dinars.

How *could* Yanya go home—even if she wanted to?

And now—quite suddenly—she did want to. A girl who could not even get a fair price for carrots and eggs was certainly not ready to venture alone into the wide world.

Sitting there by her small pile of money in the shadows of the gloomy warehouse, Yanya began to cry.

———

10

After a time the tears stopped coming.

She wiped her cheeks with her fingers, leaving streaks of dirt across her face. Then, once again, she gathered up the money in her kerchief and tied it into a knot. As she did so she noticed the careful embroidery stitching Mama had done around the edges of the kerchief—a zigzag pattern. And in the corner there were embroidered red flowers.

She felt a wave of tenderness for Mama. Busy as she was, Mama had gone to all this trouble to make Ivo's old shirt into a beautiful kerchief for *her*. Mama *must* love her, to have taken all this trouble.

Suddenly an idea exploded in her head—the answer to all her problems. She would use the hundred and two dinars to buy Mama a present. A present so splendid that Mama would forget to ask about the money Yanya had collected for the carrots and the eggs.

She ran back along the dirt road and into the street of shops that bordered the market square.

First she entered a furniture shop, which was filled with unpainted tables and chairs. A few, however, were beautifully painted in bright colors: red, orange, yellow, green. Such a chair would be the prize of their house. She pictured herself marching in the door with a fine red chair for Mama.

The shopkeeper was busy talking to a customer. Yanya waited until he had finished. Then shyly she asked the price of one red chair.

"Six hundred and fifty dinars," the shopkeeper said.

Yanya nodded.

In any case, a chair would be too difficult to carry home.

She looked at some smaller objects. Hangers, perhaps. But after all, Mama did not have many clothes. And the things she had she hung on pegs beside the door. It was more convenient.

Perhaps this fine wooden rolling pin for making meat pies—surely she had enough money for a rolling pin. Or this big wooden bowl.

But why buy the first item she came across?

The fabric shop was next door. Suddenly she knew

the answer. She would buy Mama several yards of a beautiful flowered cotton cloth so that Mama could make herself a dress and look just like a Slavonian woman. Just as beautiful. Just as grand.

The fabric shop was crowded. She looked about, found the cloth she wanted: bright green, like a field of grass planted with tiny flowers. The shopkeeper was a fat Turk who wore a black smock and a red fez. She went over to him, pulled at his sleeve. He looked down at her and smiled. He had yellow teeth.

"Please, sir," she said in a loud voice, "how much would it cost to buy seven meters of that?" She pointed to the flowered fabric.

He made some marks with chalk on a small black slate he carried. "One thousand forty dinars, mala," he said.

"Thank you," said Yanya and walked slowly from the shop.

If only she could find something really fine, which somehow did not cost very much.

Then, suddenly, she saw it. The perfect gift for Mama! It was in the window of the notions shop, surrounded by lamp shades, skeins of wool, spools of thread, scissors, stockings, and a few flowered hats—a large, bright-colored picture of St. Antun. Mama's favorite saint. Indeed, Mama had named her first-born son after St. Antun—the baby who had died in infancy.

How much, after all, could a picture cost? It was

really just paper. Mama was very religious. The picture of St. Antun would mean more to her than any amount of money Yanya might have brought home from the market. Mama could hang this beautiful picture right over her bed.

Yanya stared at the picture. "Thank you, dear St. Antun," she whispered, "for saving me." The saint stared back at her with soulful eyes. How handsome he was with his dark curly hair, his red cheeks, and the long slender fingers holding the Bible against his white robes.

She walked into the shop. This place was the most crowded of all. Bosnian, Slavonian, and Moslem women were calling out to the old shopkeeper and his boy. "Hey, *chico,* how much is this? . . . Hey, *mali,* how much are you asking for that?"

Yanya made her way through the women and planted herself in front of the shopkeeper's boy, who had many pimples on his face.

"I would like to buy," she announced in a loud voice, "I would like to buy the picture of St. Antun in the window."

He looked down at her. "All right," he said, and made his way toward the shop window. Yanya followed him. Near the window was a wooden table with—Yanya was happy to see—a pile of St. Antun pictures lying on it. The boy took the top picture, rolled it up quickly, put a string around it, and handed it to her. "Three hundred dinars," he said.

Yanya gasped.

"Do you want it or not?" the boy asked.

Yanya nodded. "I want it. Very much. But why is it so expensive?"

"Expensive?" said the boy. "For this beautiful print? It's too cheap if anything!"

"But you have so *many* here," Yanya pleaded. "Couldn't you let me have just this one for a hundred and two dinars?"

The boy looked at her as though she were mad.

"After all," Yanya added, "it's only made out of a piece of paper."

"Look," the boy said, "I'm very busy. My lowest price is two hundred eighty dinars. Do you want it or not?"

Yanya turned and walked out of the shop, her head high.

Why was everything in this world so expensive? What could she buy Mama as a present for one hundred and two dinars?

The apothecary shop was next door. There was no one inside except a tall, slim Turk dressed in a clean white smock. He was mixing powders on a small scale, but he looked up and smiled as Yanya walked in. "Hello, mala," he said. "Can I help you?"

"How many aspirin could I buy," she asked, "for a hundred and two dinars?"

"Fifty-one," he said. "They cost two dinars apiece."

She brightened a little. Fifty-one aspirin sounded like a lot. Since Mama was sick, aspirin would be a very considerate gift to bring home.

"If I take fifty-one aspirin," she said, "could you wrap them up in that nice paper?" She pointed to the stack of white paper on the counter. "I wouldn't want them wrapped just in old newspaper. They're for a present. Maybe," she added, wistfully, "you could put a colored ribbon around them, too."

The Apothecary Man smiled a little. "What kind of present is that? Fifty-one aspirin?"

"Well," said Yanya, "my mama's sick. So she probably needs aspirin. Besides, it seems to be the only present I can afford."

"Well," the Apothecary Man said, "I'm sorry but I can't sell aspirin to a child."

"But why not?" Yanya's voice squeaked upward in anxiety. "I have the money! Right here." She held up her tied kerchief.

"I'm sure you have the money," he said. "But don't you know that fifty-one aspirin could kill a person?"

"I don't want to kill my mother!" she exploded. How stupid grownups were sometimes.

He held up both hands to calm her. "I am not implying that, mala. But there are laws, you know. A pharmacist may not sell drugs to a child. In fact, some of my medicines"—he waved his arm in a grand manner toward the bottles and vials on the shelves—"some cannot be sold unless I have a prescription written by a doctor."

Yanya began to cry. She felt foolish and ashamed. It was one thing to cry alone in the warehouse where no one could see her. But to stand here in front of a stranger—sobbing! Yet she could not help herself. The tears would not stop.

The Apothecary Man came from behind the counter. He sat down on a stool and said in a kind, calm voice, "There, little one, don't cry. Tell me what's the matter. Maybe I can help."

So she told him. In between gasping, choking sobs she told him about the Moslem lady and the carrots and the eggs and the hundred and two dinars and how she wanted to bring her mama a present because she was afraid to go home.

The Apothecary Man nodded. "Look," he said, "I have an idea. The shops on the square here are quite expensive. After all, people come from miles around to do their shopping. If one customer won't buy at a high price, there's always another one who will. But," he said, "I have an old grandfather— Mad Mujo, they call him. Not that he's really mad. But he's something of a hermit. Do you know what that is?"

Yanya shook her head and wiped at her tears.

The Apothecary Man smiled. "Your face is even dirtier now than it was before you came in here." He took some cotton from a jar, spilled some strong-smelling liquid onto it. "This is alcohol," he said.

"It's very good for cleaning. Would you like me to get the dirt off?"

Yanya nodded. The alcohol smelled strong and made her eyes smart, so she closed them.

"A hermit," said the Apothecary Man, as he wiped the wet cotton over her cheeks, "is someone who likes to be alone. Someone who doesn't care for people. That's my grandfather—old Mujo. He has a little shop way back at the edge of town. No one ever goes in there. The people who come to market never venture back that far. They stay on the square. And the townspeople are afraid of him. He never goes near the mosque. So they think he's possessed by the devil. But," said the Apothecary Man, "he *does* have things to sell in his shop. Things he makes from tin. If you have the courage to walk in there, you may find a fine present for your mama."

"Oh," said Yanya. "Well, I have plenty of courage —when I have to have it."

The Apothecary Man said, "You can open your eyes now. Your face is clean—and beautiful."

It was the first time anyone had called her beautiful. She smiled at him. He smiled back. Then he took her to the door and pointed out the way to his grandfather's shop. It was down the deserted dirt road lined by warehouses.

"Tell him Alia sent you," the Apothecary Man said, "and don't be afraid of him. Not even if he mutters or screams at you. There's no devil sitting inside him. He won't hurt you."

"Thank you," Yanya said. "Thank you very much, sir."

She ran down the street, past the shops, across the road, past the tall houses, and back along the dirt road lined by the old wooden warehouses. Then there were a few wooden shacks, which seemed to be empty. Finally the road ended. There was only grass and, farther on, an old mud-brick hovel with a broken window and a door hanging off the hinge.

Could this be the house of Mad Mujo?

Even from the outside the place made her shaky with fear. How could she go *in?*

11

Yanya forced herself to walk with steady, slow steps toward the door. When she reached it she called in a quavery voice, "Hello. Is anyone there?"

No answer.

She pushed at the door, which creaked and swung open.

"Is anyone home?" she called again.

"What do you want?" A strange, shrill voice came from the corner shadows.

"Are you Mujo?" she said.

"Who told you my name? Who sent you here?" The voice shook with rage.

"Your grandson sent me," she called back. "Your grandson Alia. I want to buy something. For my mama," she added. The last sentence seemed to give her strength. She walked inside.

The old man staggered to his feet and came toward her, leaning on his cane. He looked like a devil with his long, scraggly gray beard. His brown-skinned face was furrowed deep with wrinkles. His eyes peered at her like sharp black stones.

There was one thing about him, however, that made her certain he was only an old man and not a devil. He smelled. A devil, she felt certain, would not smell so old and dirty.

"So Alia sent you here to buy something for your mama!" The old man's lips parted in a toothless smile which frightened her. "All right, child. Look around."

She did. But she could see nothing which would make a present for mama. There were only old wooden boxes piled here and there, some rusty tin cans, and a stack of yellowing newspapers beneath the small window.

Then she saw something glinting in a box. She went over to it. Inside the box were square tin graters.

She picked one up. "How . . . how much is this, sir?"

"I'll let you have it for fifty dinars," the old man said. "It's handmade," he added.

She held it toward the sunlight that spilled through the window. The grater did not look handmade. It was perfect! Just like the grater Mama borrowed from Lisa's mother in order to make apple strudel. Mama would *love* this present. And only *fifty* dinars! She could go home with the grater and with fifty-two dinars left over. Mama might think that the grater had cost as much as six hundred dinars!

"I'll take it, sir," she said.

The old man began to laugh, a chilling sound which sent shivers through her. With stiff, nervous fingers she untied her kerchief, counted out the fifty dinars into his outstretched hand, picked up the grater, and dashed out pursued by the sound of the old man's cackling laughter.

She raced down the dirt road, back to the square, across the park, and did not stop until—gasping for breath—she stood once again beside Manda. The widow was so busy chattering with a tall, black-bearded man that she barely noticed Yanya's return. Finally, however, she looked down and said, "Well, back already? Did you have a good time?"

Yanya nodded.

"What's *that?*" said Manda, pointing at the grater which Yanya had put in the empty egg basket.

"A present for mama."

Manda nodded and continued her conversation with the bearded man.

A moment later a fat Bosnian woman stopped and asked, "Mala, how much is that grater?"

Yanya looked up startled. "It's not for sale. It's a present. For my mama."

The woman nodded, and went away.

Then a Moslem lady stopped, picked up the grater, examined it carefully. "How much?" she said.

This lady looked much like the one who had cheated Yanya on the price of her eggs.

"The grater," Yanya heard herself saying, "costs a hundred dinars, madame!"

The Moslem lady flipped back her veil and Yanya saw that in fact she looked nothing at all like the lady who had cheated her. This lady had a sweet face and a soft smile. "Fine," she said. "I'll take it."

She gave Yanya the money and walked off with the grater.

For a moment Yanya felt guilty, charging this lady twice as much as the grater had cost. But the guilt was swiftly replaced by elation. She could go back, buy Mama another grater, and have a hundred and two dinars left to go home with!

"Will we be leaving soon?" she said to Manda, who was so busy talking that she paid no attention.

Yanya repeated the question in a louder voice, and Manda looked down surprised. "Home? You don't want to go home already, do you?"

"Oh, no!" Yanya exclaimed. "No, I'm having a wonderful time."

Manda nodded. "Good. Well, run along then and enjoy yourself." She turned back to the black-bearded man.

Yanya ran off across the park, through the square, and down the dirt road till she reached the house of Mad Mujo. This time she heard a hammer sounding inside. She went in and found the old man sitting on a box by a wooden table hammering at a piece of tin.

"Please, sir," she said in a loud voice, "I would

like to buy another grater." Then she added, "In fact, I'll take three of them!" Why not? She now had a hundred and fifty-two dinars. If she could sell each grater for the price the Moslem lady had paid, she would have three hundred and two dinars. That would be enough to buy Mama the St. Antun picture.

She ran back to Manda and put the graters in her egg basket.

Two Bosnian women stopped to ask the price of the graters.

"Two hundred dinars each," said Yanya and held her breath.

"I'll give you a hundred fifty," one of the women said.

Just then two Slavonian women stopped by. "Where did you get these?" one of them asked, looking down at the graters, which glinted handsomely in the sunshine.

Yanya heard herself reply, "My papa brought them back with him from Italy."

The other woman nodded. "You never can get such fine things here in this old town," she said. "How much are they?"

"Two hundred dinars each," said Yanya.

The woman nodded. "That's a fair price. I'll take all three," she said.

"Wait!" the Bosnian woman said. "*I'm* buying one of those if you don't mind!"

She took two hundred dinars from her apron

pocket and handed them to Yanya.

"All right," said the Slavonian woman. "I'll take the other two." She counted out the crumbled bills into Yanya's outstretched hand. "These will make fine presents," she said to her friend. "You can't *get* such things here any more. Not since the Communists took over."

The women walked away and Yanya, her eyes wide, her heart pounding, started counting up all the money.

"Hey! Yanya! What's going on?"

She looked up. Manda was staring at her, astonished.

"*Where* did you get all that money?"

"I . . . I sold some graters," Yanya stammered.

"And where did you get all the graters?"

"From . . . from Mad Mujo."

"Mad *who?*"

"An old man. A Moslem. Now I have to go buy some more." And before Manda could stop her, she had picked up both empty baskets and was off, racing across the park, past the shops, and down the dirt road.

This time when she burst in, Mad Mujo was sitting in a corner smoking a long pipe. There was so much smoke curling up around him that the old man looked as if he were on fire.

"Back again?" he said, emitting his shrill, cackling laugh.

But Yanya no longer felt afraid. She was too filled up with excitement. There was no room left inside her for fear.

"I would like to buy *twelve* graters!" she announced.

"Twelve?" His laughter cut off abruptly. "Twelve, you said?"

She nodded. "I have the money. Right here." She counted it out on the table before him.

The old man nodded, and slowly exhaled a puff of smoke. "Mala," he said, "you are the best customer I have had for many years." He gestured toward the box of graters with his skinny fingers. "Pick them out," he said. "Every one is a beauty."

Carefully, she selected a dozen graters. Each was shiny and well made. She put six in each basket and hurried back to the market square. This time, however, she did not return to her place beside Manda. She posted herself on the opposite side of the park. It was closer to the dirt road. Besides, she did not want Manda interfering with the sale of her tin graters.

Now, buoyed by a new flood of confidence, she started shouting out news about her wares as some of the peasant women did. "Graters! Buy a beautiful handmade grater. Very useful in the kitchen. Only two hundred and fifty dinars."

The price was so high it took her breath away. But had the Apothecary Man not told her that everyone selling on the market square put a high price on his goods?

More astounding still, within a short time she had sold all her graters for the price she asked and was on her way back to Mad Mujo's for another batch.

By the time the muezzin's singsong chant sounded out from the mosque her white kerchief was fat with dinars. She returned to the warehouse in which she had first counted out her hundred and two dinars. She now had an incredible 5752! And one grater besides. This she would give to Mama for a present.

As for the money! Half laughing, half crying, she raced back down the road, across the park, past the shops, and down the street near the Sava River. The street of Lula's shop!

"Oh, let her be there," she prayed as she ran. "Please, God, let my Lula be waiting there for me."

Lula was there!

She could see the doll as she turned the corner and ran panting into the narrow side street. She could see the splash of red color in the shop window: Lula's dress.

This time she did not stop by the window. She ran inside. The shop was empty. A fat young man sat in the corner, his feet up on a table. He was asleep.

Yanya had a pain in her side from running so fast, and she was so breathless she could hardly speak. But she managed. "Please!" she said loudly. "I have come to buy my doll."

The young man opened his eyes. He frowned at her. "What do you want, mala?"

"I have come," she said, "to buy the doll in the window."

"The doll?" He laughed. "She's not for sale."

Yanya felt that the ceiling was falling down on her head. "Not for sale?" she whispered. Then she cried out. "But she *must* be for sale. My mother came in here last year to ask the price of the doll. You told her seven thousand dinars. Or someone did. Someone told her that. The doll *must* be for sale, because I have come to buy her!" She put her white kerchief on the table and untied it.

The young man stared down in astonishment at the pile of coins and crumpled bills. "Where did you get all that?" he asked. "Did you steal it?"

"Of course not!" Yanya cried. "The money is mine. I made it by selling tin graters in the marketplace."

"Wait here," the young man said.

He went into the back room. Had he gone to get a policeman to arrest her for having so much money? But she had done nothing wrong. *Had* she? Should she have offered Mad Mujo more than fifty dinars for each grater? If only they let her have Lula, she would sell all the rest of Mad Mujo's graters and give him all the money she made.

An old man came from the back room. A Bosnian. He was smiling. He had a large blond mustache and a kind face. "So!" he said. "You want to buy the doll, mala. Do you have seven thousand dinars?"

"No," said Yanya stoutly. "But I have five thousand. In my opinion that is all she is worth. Five thousand." She held her breath while the man frowned, pulled at his ear and looked down at the pile of money on the table before him. "Please!" she prayed silently. "Oh, *please!*"

"I never really thought of selling her," the Bosnian man said. "I put her in the window for decoration. My uncle was a sailor. He brought the doll here ten years ago. Before the war. She's from Paris, France."

Paris, France! No wonder Lula was so beautiful. She came all the way from Paris, France.

"Look," said Yanya. "Men don't play with dolls, do they? What good does she do you standing there in the window? Think of all the nice things you could buy for yourself for five thousand dinars!"

The shopkeeper pulled at his other ear. Again, he frowned. Then he walked to the window, took out the doll, and stood her on the counter. "You're sure that's five thousand dinars you have in your kerchief?"

"No," she told him, her voice starting to shake. "Five thousand seven hundred and fifty-two. I need the seven hundred and fifty-two to take home to my mama for the carrots and the eggs."

The shopkeeper nodded. "Mala," he said, "I wish God had given me a smart little girl like you— instead of this lazy fat lout here." He looked at his

son, who scowled.

Then the shopkeeper counted out seven hundred and fifty-two dinars and handed the money to Yanya, along with the doll. "Be off now," he said, "before I change my mind. I never really meant to sell that doll."

Yanya stuffed the dinars in her apron pocket, put her kerchief around Lula so the doll would not get dusty on the way home, and quickly ran out of the store. She felt as if she were flying, as if this were another of her beautiful daydreams about Lula. But this time she actually had Lula! She was running down the street, back to Manda, holding Lula hard against her. She had to believe it—because it had really happened!

All the way home Manda laughed at Yanya, scolded her, criticized her. How could anyone be so stupid as to spend five thousand dinars on a *doll!*

Yanya said nothing at all. She was too busy whispering to Lula, kissing her cheek, running her fingers over the soft silk of Lula's red dress, examining the fine lace of the petticoat, feeling the doll's stiff black curls. Lula was even more wonderful than she had imagined, for when the doll was in a lying-down position her long-lashed eyes closed. And when Lula was sitting, or standing up, her wide blue eyes flew open.

"I love you so much," she whispered to Lula. "Do you know how much I love you?"

"I'm not going into the house with you," Manda

announced when they reached home. "Your mother will scream at me for letting you waste all that money on a stupid doll!" She stalked off, and Yanya entered the house alone. There was no one in the kitchen, so she ran through to the backyard and put Lula in the small wooden bed she had made for the doll in the corner of the stable.

Then she ran back to the house. Papa was still at work, of course. The boys were probably out playing soccer. She tiptoed into Mama's room. Pero was asleep in the cradle; Mama was asleep, too, her hands folded across her fat stomach. From the next room came the sound of Baka's snores.

"I'm home, Mama," Yanya whispered.

Mama opened her eyes.

"Are you feeling better, Mama dear?"

"How much money did you make?"

"Seven hundred and fifty-two dinars, Mama. I have it right here." Yanya took the money from her pocket and put the coins and bills into her mother's hands.

Her mother said nothing, but she seemed pleased.

"I brought you a present, too, Mama."

"A *present?* For *me?*" Mama sat up. "What is it?" she asked, like a child.

Yanya ran into the kitchen, took the grater from the table where she had left it, and brought it into her mother's room. "Now you won't need to borrow a grater every time you make apple strudel."

"Well," said Mama. She began to laugh. She ran her fingers over the rough center of the grater. "How pretty and shiny it is," she said. "How very pretty."

"I . . . I bought myself a present, too," said Yanya in a very soft voice. And she told Mama about the doll.

Mama let out a piercing scream.

Baka, who had been sleeping in the next room, came running in. "What is it? The baby? Is it coming already? Have the pains started?"

Mama's face had gone quite pale. She pointed at Yanya. "My daughter—" she gasped. "My daughter has spent five thousand dinars on a *doll!*"

When Baka heard the story she began to laugh. "Look," she told Mama, "money that's made easily, goes easily. That's always the way. You have your carrot and egg money. And a grater besides. What more do you want? . . . Now!" She turned to Yanya, "Let's see this Lula I've been hearing about for so long!"

They sat on Mama's double bed, and Yanya felt that they had never before been so close: Baka, Mama, and herself—all exclaiming over Lula.

They undressed her. "Look at the tiny buttons on the petticoat!" said Baka. "Imagine! These perfect little buttonholes—where no one even can see them."

"And look at the lace on the panties," said Mama. "Real French lace!"

"They know how to make things properly in Paris," Baka agreed. "Not like *this* country of Communists and peasants!"

Yanya sat quietly, saying nothing, basking in their admiration of her Lula.

That night Yanya brought in from the stable the little wooden bed she had made for Lula. She undressed the doll for the tenth time, put her daytime clothes in the chest she had made long ago, and dressed Lula in the nightgown she had sewn last year from a strip of Pero's diaper. Then she put Lula to bed. And got into bed herself.

But after a few moments, she climbed out, took Lula into her arms, and got back into bed, putting Lula on the pillow beside her. They lay then, the girl and the doll, looking up into the darkness, each with a small and contented smile.

About the Authors:

PEGGY MANN has written twenty-three popular books for young readers, including *The Street of the Flower Boxes* and *My Dad Lives in a Downtown Hotel*—both of which were filmed for television. Other titles are *The Lost Doll* (Random House) and *The Man Who Bought Himself*.

KATICA PRUSINA was born and brought up in Yugoslavia. She is now a travel agent in London. Some years ago, she lived for a time in Peggy Mann's New York City brownstone and, while there, told Ms. Mann many fascinating true stories about her childhood in Yugoslavia just after World War II. *A Present for Yanya* relates one of these stories.

About the Illustrator:

DOUGLAS GORSLINE is one of America's outstanding five artists and book illustrators. Over the years he has created the illustrations for a number of children's books, including The *Vicksburg Veteran, Viking Adventure,* and *Me and Willy and Pa.* An adult book, *What the People Wore,* for which he provided 2,800 separate pen-and-ink drawings, has become a standard reference work on costume. Mr. Gorsline is now living and working in France.